LOVE VIRTUALLY

It begins by chance: Leo receives e-mails in error from an unknown woman called Emmi. Being polite he replies, and Emmi writes back. A few brief exchanges spark a mutual interest in each other, and soon Emmi and Leo are sharing their innermost secrets and desires. The erotic tension simmers; it seems only a matter of time before they will meet in person. But they keep putting off the moment — the prospect both excites and unsettles them. And Emmi is happily married. Will their feelings for each other survive the test of a real-life commitment? And if so, what then?

DANIEL GLATTAUER

◆

LOVE VIRTUALLY

Translated from the German by
Katharina Bielenberg and Jamie Bulloch

Complete and Unabridged

ULVERSCROFT
Leicester

First published in Great Britain in 2011 by
MacLehose Press
an imprint of Quercus, London

First Large Print Edition
published 2013
by arrangement with
Quercus, London

First published in the German language as
Gut gegen Nordwind

Copyright © 2006 by Deuticke im
Paul Zsolnay Verlag Wien

English translation copyright 2011
by Katharina Bielenberg and Jamie Bulloch

British Library CIP Data

Glattauer, Daniel.
  Love virtually.
  1. Electronic mail messages- -Fiction. 2. Long-distance
  relationships- -Fiction. 3. Love stories.
  4. Large type books.
  I. Title
  833.9′2–dc23

  ISBN 978–1–4448–1497–2

Published by
F. A. Thorpe (Publishing)
Anstey, Leicestershire

Set by Words & Graphics Ltd.
Anstey, Leicestershire
Printed and bound in Great Britain by
T. J. International Ltd., Padstow, Cornwall

This book is printed on acid-free paper

1

15 January

Subject: Cancelling my subscription

I would like to cancel my subscription. Can I do so by e-mail?

Best wishes,

E. Rothner

Eighteen days later

Subject: Cancelling my subscription

I want to cancel my subscription. Is that possible by e-mail? I look forward to hearing from you.

Best wishes,

E. Rothner

Thirty-three days later

Subject: Cancelling my subscription

Dear Sir/Madam at *Like* magazine,
Are you deliberately ignoring my attempts to cancel my subscription? If you're trying to

offload more copies of your rag which, let's face it, is gradually going down the drain, I regret to inform you that I'm not going to pay another cent!

Best wishes,

E. Rothner

Eight minutes later

Re:

You've sent your message to the wrong address. This is a private one: woerter@leike.com. You want woerter@like.com. You're the third person who's sent me an e-mail trying to cancel their subscription. It must be a really shocking magazine.

Five minutes later

Re:

Oh, really sorry! And thanks for putting me right.

Best,

E.R.

Nine months later

Subject: (no subject)

Merry Christmas and a Happy New Year from Emmi Rothner

Two minutes later

Re:

Dear Emmi Rothner,

We don't know each other in the slightest but I'd like to thank you for your warm and highly original round-robin e-mail! One thing you should know: I just adore round-robin e-mails.

Rgds,

Leo Leike

Eighteen minutes later

Re:

Excuse the written imposition, Mr Rgds Leike. You seem to have slipped into my contacts list by accident — a few months ago I was trying to cancel a subscription and inadvertently got hold of your e-mail address. I'll delete you straightaway.

P.S. If you can think of a more original way of wishing people a Merry Christmas and a Happy New Year than 'Merry Christmas and a Happy New Year', please do share it with me. Until then: Merry Christmas and a Happy New Year!

E. Rothner

Six minutes later

Re:

I wish you a pleasant Christmas break and trust the forthcoming year will rank as one of your top eighty. And if, in the meantime, you subscribe to some bad times, please do not hesitate to contact me — in error — to cancel them.

Leo Leike

Three minutes later

Re:

I'm impressed!

Best,

E.R.

Thirty-eight days later

Subject: Not a cent more!

Dear Management of *Like*,

I have endeavoured to part company with

4

your magazine three times in writing and twice by telephone (I spoke to a lady called Ms Hahn). If you insist on sending it to me, I'll have to assume it's for your personal entertainment. I'd be happy to keep your enclosed bill as a souvenir so that I can continue to remember *Like* when you finally stop shipping me your latest issues. But please don't imagine for a moment that I have any intention of paying it.

Yours faithfully,

E. Rothner

Two hours later

Re:

Dear Ms Rothner,

Are you doing this on purpose? Or have you taken delivery of some bad days?

Rgds,

Leo Leike.

Fifteen minutes later

Re:

Dear Mr Leike,

Now I'm seriously embarrassed. Unfortunately I have this chronic 'ei' problem, or rather an 'e' before 'i' problem. If I'm typing quickly, and I'm trying to type 'i', somehow I always manage to slip in an 'e' before it. It's as if the tips of my two middle fingers are fighting over the keys. The left one is always trying to be that bit quicker than the right. The fact is, I was born left-handed and made to write with my right at school. My left hand hasn't forgiven me to this day. It keeps tapping out an 'e' with the middle finger before the right hand can type an 'i'. I'm so sorry to have bothered you — it (probably) won't happen again. Have a nice evening.

E. Rothner

Four minutes later

Re:

Dear Ms Rothner,

May I ask you a question? And here's a second one: How long did it take you to write your e-mail outlining your 'ei' problem?

Best wishes,

Leo Leike

Three minutes later

Re:

Two questions for you: How long do you think? And why are you asking?

Eight minutes later

Re:

I'm guessing it took you no more than twenty seconds. And I'd like to congratulate you on having produced a brilliant message in such a short period of time. It put a smile on my face. And that's something that no-one else will do this evening. As to your second question: I'm currently involved in a project on the language of e-mails. So now I'll ask you again — am I right in thinking it took you no longer than twenty seconds?

Three minutes later

Re:

Ah, so you work professionally with e-mails. Sounds fascinating, although now I feel a bit like a guinea pig. Oh well, who cares? Do you by any chance have a website? If you don't, would you like one? If you do, would you like a better one? That's my job, designing websites. (So far this has only taken me ten seconds — I've been timing it, but then again it was a work conversation, and they're always much snappier.)

I'm afraid you were completely wrong about my utterly banal 'e' before 'i' e-mail. It must have robbed me of at least three minutes of my life. I wonder what the point of it was? Now I've got a question for you: Why did you assume that my 'e' before 'i' e-mail took only twenty seconds? And before I leave you in peace once and for all (unless those guys at *Like* send me another bill), there's one more thing I'd like to know. You wrote above: 'May I ask you a question? And here's a second one: How long did it take you etc . . . ?' I've got two questions in return. First, how long did it take you to think of the joke? Secondly, is that what you call funny?

An hour and a half later
Re:
Dear unknown Ms Rothner,

I'll answer you tomorrow. I'm going to turn off my computer now.

Good evening, goodnight, whatever.

Leo Leike

Four days later

Subject: Open questions

Dear Ms Rothner,

Please forgive me for not having replied earlier, but my life is somewhat chaotic at the moment. You wanted to know why I wrongly assumed it had taken you no longer than twenty seconds to tell me about your 'ei' mistake. Well, your e-mails seem to 'effervesce', if I may be allowed to make this observation. I could have sworn that you were a fast talker and typist, a bubbly individual who cannot go about her daily business quickly enough. When I read your e-mails I can't detect any pauses. Both their tone and tempo seem to be bursting with energy — breathless, zippy, even a touch excited. Your written style is not that of somebody with low blood pressure. I imagine that your spontaneous thoughts flow into your e-mails unchecked. And then your language shows confidence; you have a skilful and deliberate way with words. But if you're telling me that it took you more than three minutes to write your 'ei'-mail, then I must have painted a false picture of you.

Unfortunately, you asked about my sense of humour. It's a sorry state of affairs. To be witty, you have to find at least one thing about yourself that's remotely funny. I can't think of anything about me that's comical at the moment, to tell the truth — I feel utterly humourless. When I look back at the past few days and weeks, all laughter escapes me. But that's my personal tale and it has no place here. Thank you, in any case, for your refreshing manner. It's been awfully nice corresponding with you. I believe all your questions have now been answered, more or less. If you happen to err into my inbox again, I'd be delighted. Just one request: Please could you cancel your *Like* subscription now? Or would you like me to do it for you?

Best wishes,

Leo Leike

Forty minutes later

Re:

Dear Mr Leike,

I have a confession to make: actually, my 'e' before 'i'-mail didn't take me longer than twenty seconds. But I was irritated that you'd presumed I was someone who just dashes off e-mails. It's the truth, of course, but you had no right to know it before now. Still, even if you have no sense of humour (at the moment), you obviously know a lot about e-mailing. I'm impressed that you managed to see straight through me! Are you a professor of literature?

Best regards,

'Bubbly' Emmi Rothner

Eighteen days later

Subject: Hello

Hello Mr Leike,

I just wanted to tell you that the folks at *Like* have stopped sending me their magazine. Did you have anything to do with it? You could e-mail me sometime, by the way. I still don't know whether you're a professor. Either Google's never heard of you, or it knows how to keep you hidden. And how's your sense of humour these days? Mind you, it's carnival time. No competition there then.

Best regards,

Emmi Rothner

Two hours later

Re:

Dear Ms Rothner,

I'm so glad you've written again — I've missed you. I was just about to get myself a

11

subscription to *Like*. (Beware, my sense of humour is coming back!) And did you really Google me? How flattering! But to be honest I'm a little disappointed that you think I might be a 'professor'. You see me as some old fart, don't you? Stiff, pedantic, a know-all. I'm not going to bust a gut trying to prove to you that I'm quite the opposite; that would only be embarrassing. But I may be writing like someone older at the moment. And I suspect that you write like somebody younger than you are. As it happens, I'm a communications consultant and a university assistant in language psychology. We're currently working on a study that's looking at the influence of e-mail on our linguistic behaviour and — the much more interesting part of the project — e-mail as a medium for conveying our emotions. This is why I tend to talk shop, but in future I promise to restrain myself.

I hope you survive the carnival festivities! My impression of you is of someone who must have quite a collection of false noses and party hooters. :-)

All the best,

Leo

Twenty-two minutes later

Re:

Dear Mr Language Psychologist,

Now it's my turn to test you (as if I haven't been doing so all along): which part of the e-mail you just sent me do you think I found most interesting, so interesting in fact that I urgently need to ask you about it?

And here's some useful advice concerning your humour: the sentence 'I was just about to get myself a subscription to *Like*' was promising — or so I thought! But when you added '(Beware, my sense of humour is coming back)', you blew it, sadly: you should have just left that out! I liked the bit about the false noses and party hooters. We've clearly got the same non-sense of humour. But trust me, I do recognize irony when I see it — spare yourself the smiley!

All the best, nice chatting to you,

Emmi Rothner

Ten minutes later

Re:

Dear Emmi Rothner,

Thanks for your humour tips. You'll make a funny man out of me yet. And I'm even more grateful for the test! It gives me the opportunity to show you that I'm not (yet) the 'self-opinionated old professor' type. If I were, then I would have guessed that the most interesting part for you must have been: 'We're currently working on a study . . . e-mail as a medium for conveying our emotions.' But I'm convinced that you're most interested in this: 'And I suspect that you write like somebody younger than you are.' Now you're forced to ask yourself: 'What makes him think he's right?' And then: 'How old does he actually think I am?' Am I right?

Eight minutes later

Re:

You're one hell of a guy, Leo Leike!!! And now you can come up with some good reasons why I must be older than my writing makes me sound. Or, more to the point: how old is my writing? How old am I? And why? If you manage to solve this puzzle, you can tell me what my shoe size is too.

All the best,

Emmi

P.S. I'm enjoying this.

Forty-five minutes later

Re:

You write like a thirty-year-old. But you're around forty, let's say forty-two. What makes me think I'm right? A thirty-year-old doesn't read *Like* on a regular basis. The average age of *Like* subscribers is around fifty. But you're younger, because you work with websites, so you could be thirty or even a fair bit younger than that. On the other hand, no thirty-year-old sends a mass e-mail to clients to wish them 'Merry Christmas and a Happy New Year'. And finally, your name is Emmi, i.e. Emma. I know three Emmas and they're all over forty. Thirty-year-olds aren't called Emma. It's only people under twenty who are Emmas again. But you're not under twenty, or you'd use words like 'cool', 'wicked', 'lush', 'totally', 'awesome' and suchlike. And you wouldn't begin sentences with capital letters, or write in full sentences either. But most importantly, you'd have better things to do than chat with a humourless man who might or might not be a professor and be interested in how young or old he thinks you might be. Another thing about 'Emmi': if your name were Emma, and you wrote as if you were younger — perhaps because

15

you felt much younger than you were — you wouldn't call yourself Emma, but Emmi. In short, my dear Emmi Rothner, you write as if you're thirty, but in fact you're forty-two. Am I right? Your shoe size is 36. You're petite, bubbly, and you've got short, dark hair. And you effervesce when you speak. Am I right?

Good evening,

Leo Leike

The next day

Subject: ???

Dear Ms Rothner,

Have I offended you? Look, I don't know you. How am I supposed to know how old you are? Maybe you're twenty, maybe you're sixty. Perhaps you're 1.9 m tall and weigh 100 kilos. Maybe your shoe size is 46 and you've only got three pairs of shoes, made to measure. And to afford a fourth pair you have to cancel your *Like* subscription and keep your website customers happy by sending them Christmas greetings. So please don't be angry with me. I had fun guessing; I have a hazy picture of you, and I've tried to convey this to you in exaggerated detail. I really didn't mean to offend you.

Best wishes,

Leo Leike

Two hours later

Re:

Dear 'Professor',

I do like your humour, it's only a semitone away from chronic seriousness, which is why it sounds particularly skewed!! I'll write again tomorrow. I'm looking forward to it already!

Emmi

Seven minutes later

Re:

Thanks! Now I can sleep peacefully.

Leo

The next day

Subject: Getting to know each other

Dear Leo,

I'm going to leave out the 'Leike' from now on. And you can leave out the 'Rothner'. I thoroughly enjoyed the e-mails you sent yesterday — I read them several times. I want to pay you a compliment. Isn't it exciting that you can get involved with someone you don't know, someone you've never set eyes on and probably never will, someone you expect nothing from, of whom you can't be sure that you'll ever get anything halfway adequate in return? That's very unusual in a man, and that's what I like about you. I just wanted to tell you that up front.

Now, a few points:

1) You have a full-on Christmas-round-robin-e-mail psychosis! Where did you pick that up? You obviously find it deeply offensive when people say 'Merry Christmas and a Happy New Year'. Fine, I promise I'll never, ever say it again. I'm amazed, by the way, that you think you can deduce my age from the way I say 'Merry Christmas and a Happy New Year'. If I'd said 'Merry Xmas and a Cool Yule', would you have thought I was ten years younger?

2) I'm sorry, Leo the Language Psychologist, but I find it a touch unworldly and fuddy-duddyish of you to say that a woman must be over twenty if she doesn't use words like 'cool', 'lush' and 'awesome'. Not that I'm desperate to write in a way

that might make you think I was under twenty, but can you really tell?

3) You say that I write like a thirty-year-old, but that thirty-year-olds don't read *Like*. Well, let me explain: the *Like* subscription was a present for my mother. So what now? Am I now younger than I write?

I'm going to have to leave you to ponder this. I'm afraid I've got an appointment (Confirmation class? Dance lesson? Manicure? Coffee morning? You choose.)

Have a nice day, Leo!

Emmi

Three minutes later

Subject: (no subject)

One other thing: you weren't so far off with the shoe size. I'm a 37. (But no shoes please, I have all the ones I need.)

Three days later

Subject: Something's missing

Dear Leo,

If you don't write to me for three days 1) I begin to wonder why, 2) I feel that something's missing. Neither is pleasant.

Please rectify!

Emmi

The next day

Subject: Sent at last!

Dear Emmi,

In my defence I confess I've written to you every day, it's just that I haven't sent the e-mails. In fact I've deleted all of them. I've reached an awkward stage in our correspondence, you see. She — this Emmi with size 37 shoes — is beginning to interest me more than befits the nature of our correspondence. And if she — this Emmi with size 37 shoes — says from the outset, 'We will probably never meet each other', then of course she's right and I agree with her. I think it's extremely wise to work on the assumption that we will never meet in person. After all, I don't want our correspondence to descend to the level of chatroom drivel or lonely hearts banter.

O.K., now I'm going to press send, so that she — this Emmi with size 37 shoes — has at least one message from me in her inbox. (The message isn't that exciting; it's only a fraction of what I wanted to write.)

All the best,

Leo

Twenty-three minutes later

Re:

Aha, so Leo the Language Psychologist doesn't want to know what Emmi with size 37 shoes looks like? I don't believe you, Leo! If a man's talking to a woman and can't see her, of course he wants to know what she looks like. Not only that, but he wants to know straightaway. Because then he'll know whether he wants to keep on talking to her. Isn't that the case?

All best,

Emmi, size 37

Eight minutes later

Re:

That was more hyperventilated than written, am I right? I don't need to know what you look like if you give me answers like that, Emmi. In any case I have you here before me. And I don't need the psychology of linguistics to achieve that.

Leo

Twenty-one minutes later

Re:

You're wrong, Mr Leo. I was as cool as a cucumber when I wrote that. You should see me when I am hyperventilating. By the way, you seem not to be answering my questions on principle, am I right? (And what do you look like when you say 'Am I right?') But if I may come back to this morning's e-mail salvo, nothing seems to make any sense. What I think you're saying is:

1) You write me e-mails and then don't send them.

2) You're gradually getting more interested in me 'than befits the nature of our correspondence'. So what does that mean? Is our correspondence not purely based on our mutual interest in complete strangers?

3) You think it's wise — no, you even think it's 'extremely wise' that we'll never meet. I envy you your passionate devotion to wisdom.

4) You don't want chatroom drivel. So what *do* you want? What should we be talking about to prevent you from becoming more interested in me than befits the 'nature' of our correspondence?

5) And finally — given the likelihood that you won't answer any of these questions — you said that your last e-mail contained only a fraction of what you wanted to write. Please feel free to write the rest, and I'll look forward to every word! Because I like reading your e-mails, dear Leo.

Emmi

Five minutes later

Re:

Dear Emmi,

It wouldn't be you without your 1) 2) 3) lists, would it? More tomorrow. Have a nice evening.

Leo

The next day

Subject: (no subject)

Dear Emmi,

Has it occurred to you that we know absolutely nothing about each other? We're creating virtual characters, piecing together identikit fantasies of each other. We're asking questions that are never answered, and that's part of the charm. We're toying with and endlessly provoking each other's curiosity by refusing point-blank to satisfy it. We're trying to read between the lines, and soon I expect we'll be trying to read between the letters. Each of us is trying desperately to build up an accurate picture of the other. And at the same time we're being meticulous in not giving away anything fundamental about ourselves. What does 'anything fundamental' mean — it means betraying nothing at all; we've yet to say anything about our lives, about our everyday existences, about the things that might be important to us.

We're communicating in a vacuum. We've politely told each other what line of work we're in. Theoretically you'd be prepared to design a nice website for me, and in return I'd draw up some (mediocre) linguistic psychograms for you. That's the sum of it. Thanks to some crummy magazine we know that we live in the same city. But what else? Nothing. There are no people around us. We don't inhabit anywhere. We don't have ages. We don't have faces. We make no distinction between day and night. We don't live in any particular time. All we've got is our computer screens — for our eyes only — and we share a hobby: we're both interested in a complete stranger. Brilliant!

Now I'll make my confession: I'm seriously interested in you, dear Emmi! I don't know why, but I *do* know that there is a clear reason for it. I also know how ridiculous my interest is. It would never survive a meeting, no matter what you look like, how old you are, how much of your considerable e-mail charm you could bring to a possible encounter, and how much of your on-screen wit you've also got in your vocal chords, your pupils, the corners of your mouth and your nostrils. I have a suspicion that this serious interest is nourished by my inbox alone. Any attempt to liberate it from there would no doubt fail miserably.

Now for the key question, dear Emmi: Do you want me to keep writing to you? (This time I'd be more than grateful for a straight answer.)

My very best wishes,

Leo

Twenty-one minutes later

Re:

Dear Leo,

That was a long one! You must be having a day off. Or does this count as work? Will you get time off in lieu? Can you offset it against tax? I've got a sharp tongue, I know. But only when I write. And only when I'm not sure of something. Leo, you make me feel unsure. But there's one thing I am sure of: yes, I want you to keep sending me emails, if you wouldn't mind. And if I've not made that clear enough, I'll say it again: YES PLEASE, MORE E-MAILS FROM LEO! MORE E-MAILS FROM LEO! MORE E-MAILS FROM LEO, PLEASE! I'M ADDICTED TO E-MAILS FROM LEO!

And now you have to tell me the truth: how can you know that there's a 'clear reason' for your interest in me without knowing what it is? You see, I don't understand what you mean, but it sounds thrilling.

All the very very best (and another very for luck), Emmi

P.S. Your last e-mail was fabulous! Totally lacking in humour, but fabulous!

Two days later
Subject: Happy Christmas

Do you know what, dear Emmi? Today I'm going to break with convention and tell you something about my life. Her name was Marlene. Three months ago I'd have written: Her name is Marlene. After five years of a present without a future I've finally ended up in the imperfect. I'll spare you the details of our relationship. The best thing about it was always starting from scratch again. Because the two of us loved starting from scratch, we did it every few months. For both of us, the other was 'the great love' of our lives. Never when we were together; only when we were trying to get back together again.

This autumn it finally came to a head: she found somebody else, someone she could imagine getting together with, and also staying together with. (Even though he's a pilot for a Spanish airline — I mean, can you believe it!?) When I found out, all of a sudden I was surer than ever that Marlene was 'the one' and I had to do everything to avoid losing her for good.

For an entire week I *did* do everything I could, and a little more besides. (Again, I'll spare you the details.) And she was actually on the verge of giving me, or rather us, one last chance: Christmas in Paris. I'd planned — go on, have a laugh, Emmi — to propose to her there. What a complete prat! She said she would just wait for the 'Spaniard' to fly in so she could tell him about me and Paris. She owed him that, she said. I felt queasy — why am I saying 'queasy'? I felt like I had a

Spanish airbus in my guts when I thought about Marlene and that pilot. That was on 19 December.

That afternoon I got — no, not even a phone call; I got a sickening e-mail from her: 'Leo, it won't work. I can't do it. Paris would be just another lie. Please forgive me!' Or something like that (No, not 'like that', those were her actual words.) I wrote back immediately: 'Marlene, I want to marry you! I really mean it. I want to be with you for ever.

I know I can make it work. We belong together. Give me one last chance. Let's talk about everything in Paris, please! Please come to Paris!'

Well, then I waited. One hour, two hours, three hours. During which I talked to her deaf-mute voice-mail every twenty minutes, read old love letters I'd saved on my computer, scrolled through the digital photos of us as a couple, taken on those countless trips when we kept getting back together. And then I stared at the screen as if possessed. My life with Marlene — my survival, as I saw it then — depended on that short, soulless ping that heralds the arrival of a new message; on that tiny, ridiculous envelope in the taskbar.

I set myself a 9.00 p.m. deadline for this torment. If Marlene had not e-mailed me by then, Paris — and with it our last chance — would be gone. It was 8.57. And then, all of a sudden, a ping, a tiny envelope (a power surge, a cardiac arrest), a message. I shut my eyes for a few seconds to gather the pathetic remains of my positive thoughts, and then focused on the message I'd been longing for: Marlene's consent, the two of us in Paris, the rest of our lives together. I opened my eyes and clicked on the message. And what did I find? 'Merry Christmas and a Happy New Year, from Emmi Rothner.'

Hence my 'full-on Christmas-round-robin-e-mail psychosis'.

Have a nice evening,

Leo

Two hours later

Re:

Dear Leo,

What a great story! Particularly impressed by the punchline. I'm almost proud to have played such a fateful role. I hope you realize that you've betrayed something extraordinary to me, your 'virtual character', your 'identikit fantasy'. That's what you might call 'private life à la Leo the Language Psychologist'. I'm far too tired to give you a useful answer today. But tomorrow you'll receive a proper analysis, if that's O.K. with you. You know, with 1.), 2.), 3.) etc. Sleep well, have some meaningful dreams. But I suggest you don't dream about Marlene.

Emmi

The following day
Subject: Marlene

Good morning Leo.

Do you mind if I get a bit tougher with you?

1) So you're a man who's only interested in a woman at the beginning and at the end: when he wants to get her, and just before he's about to lose her for good. You find the time in between — which some people call 'being together' — either too boring or too stressful, or both. Am I right?

2) By some miracle you managed to evade marriage (this time), but you'd be quite prepared to saunter up the aisle to get a Spanish airline pilot out of your soon-to-be- ex-girlfriend's bed. That testifies to something of a lack of respect for the

wedding vows. Am I right?

3) You've been married before. Am I right?

4) I can almost picture you wallowing in self-pity, sitting there reading old love letters and looking at photos instead of doing something that might make a woman believe you were capable of anything approaching love, or that you had even the slightest desire for something more permanent.

5) And then MY fateful e-mail comes flying into your inbox of destiny. It's almost as if I chose exactly the right time to say what Marlene must have had on the tip of her tongue for years: LEO, IT'S OVER, BECAUSE IT NEVER EVEN STARTED! Or to put it more subtly and poetically, more atmospherically: 'Merry Christmas and a Happy New Year, from Emmi Rothner.'

6) But then, my dear Leo, you do something pretty special. You reply to Marlene. You congratulate her on her decision. You say: YOU'RE RIGHT, MARLENE, IT'S OVER, BECAUSE IT NEVER EVEN STARTED! Or, in other words, more subtly, more energetically and forcefully, you say: 'Dear Emmi Rothner, we don't know each other in

the slightest, but I'd like to thank you for your warm and highly original round-robin e-mail! One thing you should know: I just adore round-robin e-mails. Rgds, Leo Leike.' — You're a phenomenally good loser, dear Leo — classy and magnanimous.

7) My final question: Do you want me to go on writing?

Have a good day,

Emmi

Two hours later

Re:

Hello, Emmi!

Re: 1) It's not my fault that I remind you of some man who has obviously let you down — quite stylishly even, the way you describe it. Please do not presume to know me better than you can! (You cannot know me at all.)

Re: 2) As far as my most recent evasion of the wedding vows is concerned, I can only think of myself as a 'complete prat'. But sarcastic, sanctimonious Emmi with her size 37 shoes goes one better to save the honour of marriage, presumably with eyes tightly shut while drooling at the mouth.

Re: 3) Sorry, but I've never been married! You? Several times, am I right?

Re: 4) Here's that man from point 1 again, a man who prefers to read old love letters to proving his undying love for you. Perhaps there have been many of those men in your life.

Re: 5) Yes, at that very moment when your Christmas greeting flew into in my inbox I felt as if I'd lost Marlene.

Re: 6) I replied to you back then to distract myself from my failure, Emmi. And I still consider my correspondence with you to be part of my Marlene therapy.

Re: 7) Yes, by all means feel free to write to me! Type away all your frustration with men, from the depths of your soul. Unleash all your self-righteousness, cynicism and gloating. If you feel better afterwards, my inbox has done its job. If you don't, then just treat yourself (or your mother) to another

Like subscription and unsubscribe from 'Leike'.

I hope you have a nice Monday afternoon, Leo

Eleven minutes later

Re:

Ooops! Now I've upset you. I didn't mean to, really. I thought you'd be able to take it, but I was expecting too much. I'm going to get me to a nunnery. Night night, Emmi

P.S. Re: Point 3: I've been married. And I still am!

2

One week later
Subject: C.W.
Crappy weather today, isn't it?
BW,
E

Three minutes later
Re:
1) Rain
2) Snow
3) Sleet
Rgds,
Leo

Two minutes later
Re:
Are you still upset?

Fifty seconds later
Re:

I never was.

Thirty seconds later
Re:

Perhaps you don't like chatting to married woman?

One minute later
Re:

But I do! Only sometimes I wonder why married women enjoy chatting so much to complete strangers like me.

Forty seconds later
Re:

Am I not the only woman in your inbox? How tiny a proportion of your Marlene therapy am I then?

Fifty seconds later
Re:

Well done, Emmi, you're slowly getting your touch back. Just then, you came across as a little meek and timid, and almost apathetic.

Half an hour later

Re:

Dear Leo,

In all seriousness I need to tell you how truly sorry I am for having sent you that seven-point e-mail last Monday. I've read back over it a few times since, and I have to admit it comes across as pretty vile out of context. The problem is that you have no idea what I'm like when I say such things. If we were face to face, you couldn't possibly be angry with me. (At least, that's what I imagine.) And take it from me, I'm anything but frustrated. My disappointment in men is kept in check by the natural limitations of men themselves. Meaning that of course some men are a bit limited. But I've been lucky. I'm very happy in that department. My cynicism is more playful than resentful; it doesn't come from any desire to settle scores.

That aside, I'm very touched that you've told me about Marlene. (Even though I now realize that you haven't told me anything about her at all. What kind of a woman is/was she? What does she look like? What's her shoe size? What kind of shoes does she wear?)

One hour later

Re:

Dear Emmi,

Please don't be cross with me, but I'm in no mood to tell you about Marlene's taste in shoes. Normally she'd go barefoot on the beach, that's about all I'm prepared to say. I've got to sign off now, I'm expecting someone.

Have a nice day, Leo

Three days later

Subject: Crisis

Dear Leo,

I had resolved to wait for another e-mail from you before I wrote one myself. I may not have studied language psychology, but a couple of things are chiming in my mind.

1) Between the lines I've given away that I'm not only married, but happily married to boot.

2) You reacted to this news with possibly your least enthusiastic response since our virtual togetherness began so auspiciously more than a year ago. And then you don't e-mail me again at all. Have you lost

interest in me? Have you lost interest because I'm already spoken for? And could it be that you've lost interest because I'm happily spoken for? If that's the case, you could at least be man enough to tell me.

Best wishes,
Emmi

The next day
Subject: (no subject)
LEO?

The next day
Subject: (no subject)
LEEEEEOOOOO! ARE YOU THE-ERE???????

The next day
Subject: (no subject)
Arsehole!

Two days later

Subject: A lovely message from Emmi

Hello Emmi!

I come home after an exhausting conference in Bucharest, a rather gloomy city not exactly bursting with attractions, in what they perversely refer to there as springtime (snowstorms, frosts). I switch on my computer, open the inbox and, amongst the mountain of messages ranging from the superfluous to the pathetic from 500 merciless senders, find four e-mails from Mrs Rothner — a correspondent highly esteemed for her way with words, ease of expression and bullet points. Feeling like a defrosting Romanian snow bear I'm looking forward to some nice, soulful, witty, heartwarming lines. I open the first e-mail with a sense of euphoria, and what do my eyes alight on first? 'ARSEHOLE!' What a great feeling — thanks for the welcome home!

Emmi, Emmi, Emmi! You've been doing some great hypothesizing again. But I must disappoint you. It doesn't bother me in the slightest that you're 'happily spoken for'. I'd never intended to get to know you better, better than this electronic correspondence could allow. Neither have I ever wanted to know what you look like. I'm painting my own picture of you from the messages you write. I'm constructing my very own Emmi Rothner. Your main features appear the same as they were when our contact began — it would make no difference whether you'd had three disastrous marriages, been happily divorced five times or whether you become cheerfully 'unattached' again on a daily basis, and are wild and single on Saturday nights.

Whatever is the case, I'm sad to see that contact with me is wearing you down. And there's one thing I don't understand. Why is a happily married woman (of indeterminate age) with size 37 shoes, who's not at all frustrated by men — an ironic, witty, charming and self-confident woman who's fazed by nothing — so keen to correspond with an unknown, sometimes grumpy, crisis-prone professor type, who's damaged by relationships and has an inadequate sense of humour? Why is she willing to chat about things that are so intensely personal? What, for that matter, does her husband make of it?

Two hours later
Re:

First things first: Leo the Snow Bear is back from Bucharest! Welcome home! Sorry about the 'arsehole', but it seemed the obvious thing to say. How am I supposed to know that I'm dealing with someone not of this earth, who's not in the least disappointed when he discovers that his trusty and politely sarcastic correspondent is already spoken for? Someone who'd rather create his own Emmi Rothner than get to know the real thing? If you would allow me to be the tiniest bit provocative: however convincing your fantasies, my dear Mr Language Psychologist, your creation can't possibly hold a candle to the real Emmi Rothner. Was that provocative? No? Thought not. I fear it's quite the opposite: it's you that's winding *me* up, Leo. You have this unorthodox and yet unerring way of making yourself appear more and more exciting: you want to know everything and at the same time nothing about me. Depending on your state of mind on any given day, you express either your 'serious interest' or a pathological lack of interest in me. Sometimes that's heartening, sometimes irritating. Right now I'm heartened, I have to admit. But perhaps you're one of those solitary, repressed, (Romanian) wandering grey snow wolves who can't look a woman in the eye. A man who has a terrible fear of real-life encounters. Someone who is forever constructing his own realms of fantasy because he cannot find his way in the living, tangible, real world. Perhaps you've got a genuine complex about women. I'd love to ask Marlene about that. You don't by any chance have a telephone number for her, or for the Spanish pilot? (Joke! Don't disappear in another three-day huff.)

It's just that I've got a crush on you, Leo. I like you. I like you very much! Very very very much! And I just can't understand why you wouldn't want to know what I look like. I'm not suggesting that we *should* see each other. Of course we shouldn't! But I have to say I wouldn't mind knowing what you look like. It would explain a lot. I mean, it would explain why you write the way you do. Because then you'd look like someone who writes the way you do. I'd badly like to know what someone who writes the way you do looks like. And that would explain it.

Talking of explaining things: I don't want to tell you about my husband. You're welcome to tell me about all your girlfriends (if you've got any that aren't in your inbox). I could give you some good advice; I'm brilliant at empathizing with women, because I am one, after all. But my husband . . . O.K., I'll tell you: we have a fantastic, harmonious relationship and two children (he was kind

44

enough to bring them with him, to spare me the pregnancies). We don't really keep secrets from each other. I've told him that I've been e-mailing 'a nice language psychologist'. He asked me whether I wanted to meet you. I said I didn't. Then he said: So what's it all about? I said: Nothing. He said: I see. And that was it. He didn't ask any more questions, and I didn't want to tell him more either. I don't want to talk about him any further, O.K.?

So, dear snow bear, over to you: What do you look like? Tell me. Please!!!

All the best,

Emmi

The next day

Subject: Test

Dear Emmi,

I'm finding it hard to resist your hot-and-cold e-mails. Who's actually paying us for the time we're whiling away here together (or not together)? And how can you fit it in with your career and your family? I assume that your two children have at least three chipmunks or similar to keep them busy. Where do you find the time for such an intense and full-on correspondence with a strange snow bear?

45

So you're set on knowing what I look like? O.K., here's a suggestion. I propose a game. A mad game, admittedly, but you ought to get to know another side of me. I bet that out of, let's say, twenty women I could identify the one and only Emmi Rothner, whereas you'd never guess the real Leo Leike among the same number of men. Do you fancy having a go at this experiment? If you agree we'll work out how we do it.

Have a nice afternoon,

Leo

Fifty minutes later

Re:

Definitely, let's do it! What a daredevil you are! This is what I think, but you're not to hold it against me: I don't think I'm going to find you at all attractive, dear Leo. Almost definitely not, as I don't find that many men good-looking apart from a few exceptions (mostly gay). Quite the opposite — but I don't want to go into that now. So you think you'll be able to recognize me straight off? In that case you must already have a mental image of me. What was it you said? 'Forty-two years old, petite and bubbly, short dark hair'. Well, good luck to you if you think you'll spot me from that! So how should we do this? Shall we send each other twenty photos, with one of ourselves amongst them?

All the best,

Emmi

Two hours later

Re:

Dear Emmi,

I suggest that we meet in person without knowing it, i.e. we should stay in a crowd. We could go to Huber, for example, the big café in Ergelstrasse. You must know it. There's always a very mixed crowd in there. We could choose a window of two hours — perhaps on a Sunday afternoon? — when we'd both have to be there. If there's a constant stream of people coming and going we won't draw attention to the fact that we're trying to work each other out.

As for possible disappointment on your part — if my appearance doesn't tick all the boxes — maybe even after our encounter we shouldn't reveal what we really look like. The most interesting thing is whether and how one of us thinks we've recognized the other, not what we both actually look like. I'll say it again: I don't want to know what you *look like*. I just want to recognize you. And I will. What's more, I no longer think my earlier picture of you is accurate. You seem to have shed a few years (despite husband and children), Mrs Emma Rothner.

And there's another thing. I love the way you keep on quoting from my old e-mails. It must mean that you haven't deleted them. How flattering!

What do you think about my meeting idea?

All the best,

Leo

Forty minutes later

Re:

Dear Leo,

There's just one problem: if you work out which one's me, you'll know what I look like. If I work out who you are, I'll know what you look like. But you don't want to know what I look like. And I'm worried that I won't like the way you look. Will that be the end of our exciting journey together? Or to put it another way: is this sudden desire to identify each other an excuse not to send e-mails any more? I would find that too high a price to pay for my curiosity. I'd rather remain anonymous and get e-mails from the snow bear for the rest of my life.

Kiss, Emmi

Thirty-five minutes later

Re:

Nicely put! I'm not worried about our meeting. You won't recognize me. And I've got such a clear picture of you that it needs only to be confirmed. Should my picture of you (contrary to all expectations) be inaccurate, however, I won't work out who you are anyway. Then I can preserve my fantasy image.

A kiss from me, too,

Leo

Ten minutes later

Re:

Maestro Leo,

It's driving me nuts that you're so sure you know what I look like! In fact I think it's downright impertinent. One more question: when you gaze at your high-res fantasy image of me, do you at least like what you see?

49

Eight minutes later

Re:

Like, like, like. Is that really so important?

Five minutes later

Re:

Yes, it's crucial, Mr Moral Theologian. Well, for me it is anyway. I like 1) to like. And I like 2) to be liked.

Seven minutes later

Re:

Is it not enough 3) to like yourself?

Eleven minutes later

Re:

No, I'm far too narcissistic for that. Anyway, it's easier to like yourself if you know that other people like you too. You probably just want 4) to make your inbox happy, am I right? Your inbox is a tolerant sort. You don't have to brush your teeth for your inbox. Do you still have all your own teeth, by the way?

Nine minutes later

Re:

At last, I've got Emmi's blood racing again. To close the subject for the time being, I really do like my fantasy image of you — if I didn't, I wouldn't think of it so often, dear Emmi.

One hour later

Re:

So you think of me often? That's nice. I think of you often too, Leo. Maybe we shouldn't meet up after all. Night night!

The next day

Subject: Cheers!

Hello Leo,

Sorry to disturb you so late. Are you online? Fancy a glass of red wine? Not to share, obviously. I should tell you that I'm already on my third. (If you don't drink wine, please lie and tell me that you enjoy a glass from time to time, or a bottle, all in moderation. You see, there are two kinds of men I can't abide: drunks and ascetics.)

Fifteen minutes later

Subject: (no subject)

I'm just about to drink my fourth, and then I'll pass out. Your last chance for today.

Seven minutes later

Subject: (no subject)

Shame. Your loss. Thinking of you. Night night.

The next day

Subject: Shame

Dear Emmi,

I'm really very sorry to have missed our romantic midnight assignation at our computers. I'd have drunk a glass with you in flash, to you and to virtual anonymity. Would white wine have been O.K. too? I prefer white to red. No, fortunately I don't have to lie to you. I'm not often drunk, and nor am I always monk-like. O.K., I'd ten times rather be drunk than ascetic; ten times over, and twenty times more often. Take Marlene (remember her?), Marlene never touched a drop of alcohol. She couldn't take it. And what was worse, she couldn't take it when I drank a single drop either. Do you know what

I mean? That's when you start living at cross purposes. When it comes to drinking, it's got to be both of you or neither.

As I said, it's a real shame that I wasn't able to take up your enticing offer yesterday evening. I'm afraid I got home far too late. Another time.

Your online-drinking-buddy-to-be,

Leo

Twenty minutes later

Re:

Home far too late? Leo, Leo, where have you been, gadding about in the night? Don't tell me a Marlene successor has turned up. If that's the case, you're going to have to tell me all about her right now, so I can put you off. You see, all my instincts tell me that you shouldn't be getting involved with anyone at the moment, you're not ready for another relationship. And anyhow, you've got me. Your fantasy of me must come much closer to your concept of the ideal woman than someone you've met in a bar (for bachelor snow-bearish professor types) with red plush seats at two in the morning, or however late it was. So from now on please stay at home, and from time to time we can drink a glass of wine together around midnight (yes, it can be white wine in your case). And then you'll get tired and go to bed, leaving you rested the next day, ready to send more e-mails to Emmi Rothner, your imaginary goddess. Does that sound like a plan?

Two hours later

Re:

Dear Emmi,

How wonderful to be able to experience the beginnings of another truly enchanting outburst of jealousy! That sounds rather Italian, I know, but I enjoyed it anyway. As for my relationships with women, why don't we give them the same treatment as your husband, two children and the six chip-munks. Here's not the place! Here there's just the two of us — for the two of us. We'll stay in contact until one of us runs out of steam or loses the will. I don't think it'll be me.

Enjoy this lovely spring day,

Leo

Ten minutes later

Re:

I've just remembered — what's happened to our recognition game? Don't you want to do it any more? Should I be worrying about your bleary-eyed plush bar squeeze? What about the day after tomorrow, Sunday 25 March, from 3 p.m. in Café Huber? It'll be really busy. Let's do it!

Emmi

Twenty minutes later

Re:

Of course, dear Emmi. I look forward to picking you out. But I've already got this weekend planned. Tomorrow I'm off to Prague for three days — strictly 'for pleasure', so to speak. But how about indulging in our parlour game next Sunday?

One minute later

Re:

Prague? Who with?

Two minutes later
Re:

No, Emmi, just don't.

Thirty-five minutes later
Re:

O.K., do what you like (or don't like). But don't come running to me afterwards with your love problems! Prague is just perfect for love problems, especially at the end of March: everything's grey, and at night you have anaemic dumplings and dark beer in some pub that's wood-panelled in the darkest shade of brown imaginable, watched over by an under-employed, depressive waiter whose reason for living stopped with Brezhnev's state visit. It's all over after that. Why don't you go to Rome instead? It's nearly summer there. I'd fly to Rome with you.

So our game will have to wait a while longer. On Monday I'm going skiing for a week. I don't mind telling you who I'm going with, my trusted correspondent: with one husband and two children (but no chipmunks!). The neighbours are going to look after Wurlitzer. Wurlitzer is our overweight tomcat. He looks just like a jukebox, but he always plays the

56

same tune. And he hates skiers, which is why he's staying at home.

Have a lovely evening.

Emmi

Five hours later

Re:

Are you home yet, or are you still hanging out in that plush bar?

Night night,

Emmi

Four minutes later

Re:

I'm back home. I've been waiting for Emmi to check up on me. Now I can go to bed in peace. I'm off early in the morning, so I hope you and your family have a good week's skiing. Goodnight. Read you soon!

Leo

Three minutes later

Re:

Are you wearing pyjamas?

Goodnight,

E

Two minutes later
Re:

Do you sleep naked, by any chance?
Do you . . . ?
Goodnight,
Leo.

Four minutes later
Re:

Hey there, Mr Leo, that was really quite erotic. I didn't think you were up to it. I've no desire to dispel the prickling tension that's emerging between us, so I'd better not ask what your pyjamas are like. Goodnight then, and have a good time in Prague!

Fifty seconds later
Re:

Well, *do* you sleep naked?

One minute later
Re:

He really wants to know! For the purposes of your fantasy world, my dear Leo, let's say it depends on who I'm sleeping with. Hope you two have a good time in Prague!

Emmi

Two minutes later

Re:

You three, you mean! I'm going with an old friend and her partner.

Leo

P.S. I'm shutting down now.

Five days later

Subject: (no subject)

Dear Emmi,

Are you online there, skiing?

Best wishes,

Leo

P.S. You were right about Prague — my two chums decided to split up. But it would have been worse in Rome.

Three days later

Subject: (no subject)

Dear Emmi,

It's high time you came back. I'm missing being under e-mail surveillance. Evenings hanging around in plush bars are no fun at all now.

One day later

Subject: (no subject)

Just so you've got three messages from me in your inbox.

All the best,

Leo

P.S. Yesterday I bought a new pair of pyjamas especially for you, well, with you in mind.

Three hours later

Subject: (no subject)

Are you not writing to me?

Two hours later

Subject: (no subject)

Can't you write to me any more, or don't you want to write?

Two and a half hours later

Subject: (no subject)

I can change the pyjamas if that's the problem.

Forty minutes later

Re:

Oh Leo, you're so sweet!! But there's no point in us carrying on like this. This is so far removed from real life. My skiing holiday: now that was real life. It might not have been the best, but it was good enough and I have to confess I wouldn't want it any other way. So that's how it is, and however it is, it's fine by me. The kids got on my nerves somewhat, but that's what kids are for. Besides, they're not mine, and every now and again they reproach me for that. But the holiday went pretty much O.K. (I've already said that, haven't I?)

Let's be honest with each other, Leo: as far as you're concerned I'm just a fantasy image. The only real thing about me is a few letters that you, with all your language psychology, might be able to bring together into some kind of harmonious whole. To you I'm like telephone sex, only without the sex and without the telephone. Computer sex then, but again, without the sex or the downloadable

61

images. And for me you're just a bit of fun, a way for me to refresh my flirting skills. You allow me to do the one thing I've been missing: I can experience the first stages of an affair (without actually having to have an affair). But we two beauties are already on the second or third stage of an affair that cannot happen. So I think it's about time we stopped where we are. Otherwise the whole thing will become ridiculous. We're not fifteen any more, even if I'm much closer to it than you are, but either way we're not, and there's nothing we can do about that.

There's something else I want to say, Leo. Throughout the whole of our family skiing holiday, which was irritating at times, but overall really nice, peaceful, harmonious, funny, even romantic, I couldn't help thinking of a certain snow bear called Leo Leike, whom I've never met. That's just not right. It's actually pretty sick, don't you think?

Shouldn't we just call it a day? asks Emmi.

Five minutes later

Re:

One other thing: shame about your friends. You're right: Rome would probably have been hellish.

Two minutes later

Re:

So what are your new pyjamas like?

The next day

Subject: Meeting up

Dear Emmi,

Can't we at least play our 'recognition game'? Maybe after that we'll find it a little easier to break off our 'affair that cannot happen'. Even if I stop writing to you and waiting for your e-mails, Emmi, it doesn't mean I won't be thinking of you. That would be so shabby and calculating. Let's still do the experiment! What do you think?

All the best,

Leo

P.S. I can't describe my new pyjamas; you'd have to see them and feel them.

An hour and a half later

Re:

Next Sunday between 3 and 5 p.m. at Café Huber?

Best wishes,

Emmi

P.S. Leo, Leo, what you said about the pyjamas, 'you'd have to see them and feel them', that's what I call a come-on. If it hadn't been you writing, I might even have said it was a particularly blatant come-on!

Fifty minutes later

Re:

That sounds good! But we can't turn up dead on three and leave the café at five on the dot. And we mustn't look for each other too obviously. Most important of all, don't do anything so conspicuous that it might give the game away. If you do identify me, you mustn't get carried away and then rush up to me and say, 'You're Leo Leike, aren't you?' We really should give ourselves the opportunity to *not* recognize each other. Don't you think?

Eight minutes later

Re:

Yes, yes, yes, have no fear, Mr Language Professor, I won't come too near. And to avoid further confusion, I suggest we have an e-mail embargo until Sunday. We can write to each other again afterwards, O.K.?

Forty seconds later
Re:
O.K.

Thirty seconds later
Re:
Which doesn't mean that you should stay out late every night between now and then, boozing in some plush bar.

Twenty-five seconds later
Re:
Of course I won't! Anyway, it's only fun if Emmi Rothner takes me to task on an hourly basis on the off chance that I might be.

Twenty seconds later
Re:
O.K., you've reassured me. Till Sunday then!

Thirty seconds later
Re:
Until Sunday!

Forty seconds later
Re:

Don't forget to brush your teeth.

Twenty-five seconds later
Re:

You always have to have the last word, don't you, Emmi?

Thirty-five seconds later
Re:

Generally, yes. But if you answer again now, I'll let you have it.

Forty minutes later
Re:

A footnote to my pyjamas. I wrote, 'You'd have to see them and feel them.' You replied that this would be a blatant come-on had anybody else written it. I wish to object. I demand that in future you credit my blatant come-ons as just that, as blatant as the next man's. Allow me to be as blatant as I am. Back to the point: you really have to feel my pyjamas, they're sensational. Give me your address and I'll send a sample. (Is that blatant too?) Goodnight!

Two days later

Subject: Discipline

I take my hat off to you, Emmi, you've really got discipline! See you the day after tomorrow, Café Huber.

Yours,

Leo

Three days later

Subject: (no subject)

Hi Leo, were you there?

Five minutes later

Re:

Of course I was!

Fifty minutes later

Re:

Shit! I was afraid of that.

Thirty seconds later

Re:

What were you afraid of, Emmi?

Two minutes later

Re:

Every man who could conceivably have been Leo Leike was a total no-no. To look at, I mean. I'm sorry, that might sound a little harsh, but I'm giving it to you straight. Seriously, Leo, were you really at Café Huber between three and five yesterday? And I don't mean hidden away in the loos or entrenched in some building across the road, but actually at the bar or in the lounge, standing or sitting, squatting or kneeling, whatever?

One minute later

Re:

Yes Emmi, I really was there. Which of the men did you think might have been Leo Leike, may I ask?

Twelve minutes later

Re:

Dear Leo,

I don't feel comfortable going into details. But tell me you weren't that — how can I put it? — stocky gentleman, well, stunted, let's be honest, with all-over body hair that looked like a brillo pad? He was wearing a T-shirt which was once white, a mauve skiing jumper tied around his waist, and was standing at one end of the bar drinking a Campari or some other red concoction. I mean, if that *was* you, all I can say is this: each to his own. I'm sure there are plenty of women who would find a guy like that utterly fascinating, even irresistibly attractive. I've no doubt that one day you'll find a woman to spend the rest of your life with. But I have to be frank: you wouldn't be my type, sorry to say.

Eighteen minutes later

Re:

Dear Emmi,

All respect to your disarming and revealing honesty. But 'not offending people' is not one of your strengths. It's clear that looks really are your highest priority. You're behaving as if your future love life depended on how physically attractive you find your e-mail friend. But first let me reassure you that the hairy beast at the bar — he and I are not one and the same person. But go ahead, feel free to continue with the descriptions — who else might I have been? And second, a related

69

question: If I'm one of the no-nos, does that signal the end of our exchanges?

Thirteen minutes later
Re:

No, Leo, we can go on e-mailing each other with abandon. You know me: I'm prone to wild exaggeration. I'm getting all excited, and I don't want my flow interrupted. The fact is, I didn't see a single man at the café yesterday I thought could be even half as exciting as the way you write to me. And that's precisely what I was afraid of. Not one of those dreary Sunday-afternoon faces in Café Huber came remotely close to the way you write to me: shy and attentive on the one hand, on the other sure-footed and forthright, charmingly snow-bearish and once in a while even sensual, but always uncannily sensitive.

Five minutes later
Re:

Really, not one? Perhaps you just missed me.

Eight minutes later

Re:

Dear Leo,

You've given me renewed hope. But sadly I don't think I've overlooked anyone who didn't deserve to be overlooked. I found the two pierced freaks sitting at the third table on the left quite sweet. But they couldn't have been more than twenty. There was an interesting-looking guy, maybe the *only* interesting-looking guy, standing with one of those leggy blonde, angel-vamp model types at the bar towards the back on the right. They were holding hands, and he only had eyes for her. Then there was another quite nice-looking man — looked like a rowing champ, built like a Give Way sign — but he had an unfortunate moronic grin. No, Leo, that definitely wasn't you! So who else was there? Lawn-mowing and allotment enthusiasts, men who collect beer mats and have shares in breweries, chaps in dark suits with briefcases, D.I.Y. fanatics with fingers that look as if they've been mutilated in a wrench. Guys who go windsurfing, with childishly dreamy faces, permanent kids in other words. But not one charismatic man to be seen. Hence my bold question: which of these was my language psychologist? Which one was my

Leo Leike? Did I lose him to Café Huber on this fateful Sunday afternoon?

An hour and a half later
Re:

Without wishing to sound arrogant, my dear Emmi, I knew that you wouldn't identify me!

Forty seconds later
Re:

WHICH ONE WERE YOU LEO? TELL ME!!!

One minute later
Re:

Let's talk again tomorrow, Emmi, I've got to meet someone now. And you ought to thank the good Lord that you've already found a man for life. By the way, just a minor observation: Has it occurred to you that we haven't talked about you at all? Which one could Emmi Rothner have been? More tomorrow.

Lots of love, yours,

Leo

Twenty seconds later

Re:

What?? You can't just go now? Leo, you can't do that to me! Write back! Now! Please!

An hour and a half later

Re:

He's not writing back. Perhaps he was the hairy beast after all . . .

3

The next day
Subject: Nightmare
Leo Leike, I've got it!! I've just woken up in a cold sweat. I've worked it out! That was beautifully contrived, and you knew all along I'd never guess. No wonder: YOU WERE A WAITER! You know the guy who runs the place and he let you pretend to be a waiter for a couple of hours, am I right?

Fifteen minutes later
Re:

And? Are you disappointed? (Hello, by the way.)

Eight minutes later
Re:

Disappointed? Deflated, more like! Peeved! Pissed off! Pranked! You've stitched me up and I feel cheated. And you've been planning this nasty little trick all along. You're the one who suggested that we meet in Café Huber. The entire staff has

74

probably been laughing their heads off at my expense for weeks. I think it's really shabby and nasty of you. It's not the Leo Leike I know. It's not the Leo Leike I've come to know. It's not the Leo Leike I might have got to know better! And I've no intention of getting to know that Leo one iota more! In one fell swoop you've trashed everything we've spent months building up. Goodbye!

Nine minutes later
Re:
So do you at least like me, I mean to look at?

Two minutes later
Re:
Do you want an honest answer? I'll gladly give you one, as a parting shot.

Forty-five seconds later
Re:
If it's not too much trouble — that would be nice.

Thirty seconds later

Re:

I don't think you're good-looking. I don't even think you're ugly. I think you're just nothing. Boring as hell. Totally uninteresting. Just BLEEUGHH!!

Three minutes later

Re:

Really? That sounds pretty harsh. I'm glad I'm not in that man's skin. And I wasn't in his waiter's outfit either. I wasn't him, I'm not him, and I probably never will be him either. And I wasn't any of the waiters. I wasn't a delivery man or a kitchen porter. I wasn't a policeman in uniform. I wasn't the loo attendant. I was plain old Leo Leike, a customer in Café Huber on Sunday after-noon between three and five. Too bad about your sleep, dear Emmi 'looks-are-everything' Rothner. Too bad about your wasted nightmare.

Two minutes later

Re:

Thank you, Leo!!! Now I need a whisky.

Fifteen minutes later

Re:

I suggest that we talk about you instead, to give your nerves a break. I'm going to assume that, even if I find a woman's looks rather important, they cannot be anywhere near as important as a man's looks are for you. And with this more flexible approach, I concluded that at the appointed time there were a remarkably large number of interesting women in the café who could have fitted the bill.

(I have to break off briefly. We've got a conference — I do a bit of work on the side, you know, although I may not be able to afford myself this luxury soon.)

I'll be back in a couple of hours, and we'll resume, if that's O.K. Incidentally, I suggest you put the lid back on the whisky bottle now . . .

Ten minutes later

Re:

1) I simply can't comprehend how a man who can create such intimacy with words, to the extent that he can sense Emmi in

77

her most private moments (as she drinks whisky), I mean, I just don't get how someone who writes like that could look anything like one of those men I saw with my own eyes in Café Huber! So I'm going to ask you one more time, dear Leo: is it possible that I simply overlooked you? Please say yes! I don't want you to be one of those types I described yesterday. What a shame that would be!

2) Maybe there weren't that many 'remarkably interesting women' in the café. Maybe it's just that Mr Leike has a remarkable interest in (a remarkably large number of) women.

3) Still, I wouldn't mind changing places with you. From a 'remarkably interesting' selection, you can pick out the fantasy Emmi Rothner of your desires — whichever one takes your fancy. While I'm stuck with a Leo Leike I managed not even to notice, and that's my best-case scenario. Not exactly a recommendation.

4) You obviously don't have a clue which one I was. All yours, then!

Two hours later

Re:

Thank you, Emmi, at last another Rothner list. Do you mind if I cut straight to point 4)? If you think I have no idea who you are, then you're seriously mistaken. I must confess, on the other hand, that I don't know *exactly* who you are. There are just three possibilities, and I'm convinced that you're one of these women. If it's all the same to you, I'm going to use letters rather than numbers to order my three types. I don't want the whole thing to look like an awards ceremony with podium places. So here are my Rothner candidates:

A) The prototype, the Ur-Emmi. She was standing at the bar, fourth from the left. Around 1.65m, petite, short dark hair. Just under forty. Hectic and nervous, rapid movements, endlessly twirling her whisky glass (!!), seemed a bit lofty, looking down her nose at everything (a dignified arrogance masking a slight insecurity). Trousers, coat: funky dress-sense. Funny felt handbag. Green shoes that looked as though they were chosen from a collection of a hundred others for that Sunday afternoon. (About size 37!!!) Looked at men the way you might try to without them noticing. Facial features: fine, a little unrelaxed. Face: beautiful. Type: boisterous, buzzing, temperamental. In other words, a classic Emmi Rothner type.

B) The alternative model, the Blonde-Emmi. Changed her seat three times, started out at the front on the right, then right at the back, then in the middle. In the end spent a short time at the bar. Very confident, a little slower in her movements (than the Ur-Emmi). Blonde, straggly hair, 1980s style. Around thirty-five. Drinks: coffee followed by red wine. Smoked a cigarette. (Looked as if she really enjoyed it, but didn't seem addicted.) Height: a good 1.75m. Long, slim legs. Red, branded trainers. (About size 37!!!) Faded jeans, tight black T-shirt (large breasts, if I may make such an observation). Looked at men very casually. Facial features: relaxed. Face: beautiful. Type: feminine, self-confident, cool.

C) The anti-type, the Surprise-Emmi. Kept on wandering around the café, stood at the bar a number of times. Very shy. Exotic complexion, large, almond eyes, avoided eye contact, seemed unsociable. Shoulder-length, brunette hair, layered at the front. Around thirty-five. Drinks: coffee, mineral water. Height, roughly 1.70m. Slim, wonderful black-and-yellow trousers (certainly not cheap), casual, dark ankle-boots. (Shoe size about 37!!!) Distinctive chunky wedding ring! Gazed about as if she were searching for something, and gave the impression of being dreamy, beatific, melancholic, even a little sad. Facial features: soft. Face: beautiful. Type: feminine, sensual, diffident, shy. And, because of all this, maybe Emmi Rothner.

So, dear Emmi, I can offer you these three. Maybe I'll leave you with an answer to your pressing question number 1): whether you might have overlooked me. Yes, of course you might have. But I'm afraid you didn't.

Yours,
Leo

Five hours later

Re:

Dear Emmi,

Am I not going to get another e-mail from you today? Are your powers of perception so poor? Do you no longer care whether I spend all night hanging around in plush bars? (Or with whom?)

Goodnight,
Leo

The next day

Subject: Most puzzling

Hello Leo,

You're wearing me out — I can't think about anything else! I liked the way you described those women! I'm stunned; you never cease to amaze me. I just wish I hadn't seen you!!! Let's assume I am one of those three women: how could you have observed me so closely without immediately giving yourself away? Did you have a video camera on you? Or rather: if I had been one of those three, I must have got a good look at you too. And if I did, then this confirms my suspicion that you were one of those men who just can't be Leo Leike, because — forgive me! — they looked as boring as hell. Secondly (no numbers today, just words. You've been so free with numbers that all you're missing are the vital statistics): Why those three in particular?

Thirdly, which was your favourite?

Fourth, tell me which one you were, please! Give me a little clue, at least.

With friendly greetings,

Yours impatiently,

Emmi

Re:

Why those three in particular? Emmi, it's been clear to me for a long time that you're what you might call a 'damned good-looking woman'. Because you know you're good-looking, damn it. You're forever letting on that you know you're good-looking. You write it between the lines, and sometimes in the lines too. No woman would go on like this unless she knew 100 per cent that men found her attractive. As an 'interesting woman', you're even put out if you don't leave every other woman for dust. Let's go back to your point 2) from yesterday. You wrote, 'Maybe there weren't that many 'remarkably interesting women' in the café. Maybe it's just that Mr Leike has a remarkable interest in (a remarkably large number of) women.' You must consider yourself the most interesting of all, and it's almost an affront to you if you're not recognized as such. I had it easy; all I had to do was keep my eye out for attractive women who appeared to be looking for someone (whether subtly or not), and who might have had size 37 shoes. And those three fitted the bill.

Regarding your third point, it's irrelevant which of the three I preferred. All were attractive in their own way, but I believe all three of them to be happily married with two children, and if not six chipmunks then at least with a cat called Wurlitzer. For me, all three inhabit another world into which I can peer virtually, but which I will always be forbidden to enter. I've said many times that I prefer to paint my Emmi Rothner in my mind (or on the computer screen) rather than chase after her or mourn for her in the real world. I admit, however, that Emmi number 1), the Ur-Emmi, seems to me to be the most authentic, and to match most closely the Rothner who writes to me.

As to your fourth point, if you concede that you are one of my three Emmi candidates, then I'll give you a clue as to who I may have been.

Love,

Leo

Twenty minutes later

Re:

O.K., Leo. But you give me your clue first, and then I'll tell you if you're right or not.

84

Three minutes later

Re:

Do you have brothers or sisters?

One minute later

Re:

Yes, an older sister who lives in Switzerland. Why? Was that the clue?

Forty seconds later

Re:

Yes, that was the clue, Emmi.

Twenty seconds later

Re:

But that doesn't tell me anything!

One minute later

Re:

I've got an older brother and a younger sister.

Thirty seconds later

Re:

That's fascinating, Leo. But can we talk about them another time? Right now I'm concentrating on who the brother of this older brother and younger sister might be.

Fifty minutes later

Re:

Leo, hello, where are you? Are you trying to keep me in suspense?

Eight minutes later

Re:

I see my sister Adrienne a lot. We're very close. We tell each other everything. So, dear Emmi, that was a massive clue. You'll have to work the rest out for yourself. So were you one of my three Emmis?

Forty seconds later

Re:

That's cryptic, Leo! Please give me ONE more hint! And then I'll tell you.

Thirty seconds later

Re:

Why don't you ask me what my sister looks like?

Thirty-five seconds later

Re:

What does your sister look like?

Twenty-five seconds later

Re:

She's tall and blonde.

Thirty seconds later

Re:

O.K., that's nice, whatever, I give up!

Dear Leo, language psychologist, people watcher: I AM ONE OF THOSE THREE. But from the way you describe them, these three women with apparently the same shoe size could hardly be more different. I'm amazed you could find all three attractive and interesting-looking at the same time. But that's men for you.

I hope you have a pleasant evening. I'm going

to take a Leo-break. It's about time I turned to more essential matters.

Bye-bye,

Emmi

An hour later

Re:

Just then you were totally Ur-Emmi, number 1.

Five hours later

Re:

My sister is a model.

Goodnight.

The next day

Subject:!!!!!!

NO WAY!

Forty-five seconds later

Re:

Oh yes.

Forty seconds later
Re:
The long-legged blonde angel-vamp model?

Twenty-five seconds later
Re:
That's my sister!

Three minutes later
Re:
So you were the guy holding her hand, looking into her eyes so lovingly!

One minute later
Re:
That was just a cover. She spent the whole time looking at women and describing all the potential Emmis in minute detail.

Forty seconds later
Re:
Shit, now I can't remember what you look like! I glanced at you only very briefly.

Fifteen minutes later

Re:

At least I've salvaged the honour of all the men in the café that afternoon. How did you describe me? 'The only interesting-looking guy, standing with one of those leggy blonde angel-vamp model types at the bar.' I'm going to print that out and frame it!

Ten minutes later

Re:

I wouldn't get too excited, sweetheart. Basically, all I saw was that extremely beautiful, rather cool blonde. And I thought to myself: anyone who's with a woman like that must be an interesting guy. All I know about you is that you're fairly tall, fairly slim, fairly young, fairly well-dressed. And as far as I remember you also have a fair supply of hair and teeth. The thing that really struck me was the expression on the face of your supposed lover, your sister. She was looking at you as you would only look at someone you love and cherish deeply. But maybe it was just an act, to put Emmi Rothner off the scent. I have to say that was a highly intelligent ploy, to turn up there with your sister. I'm glad you talk to her about me. It makes me feel good. I think you're alright, Leo! (And I'm ecstatic that you're not the hairy beast, nor anyone else from Café Huber's cabinet of horrors.)

Half an hour later

Re:

And I don't have a clue what you look like either, my dear. I spent the whole time standing with my back to the Emmi candidates Adrienne had picked out. She described the women to me from 'a woman's perspective', hence all the fashion details. I didn't see a thing with my own eyes.

One hour later

Re:

Just one more question before we conclude our clever little game: which Emmi did your sister like the most, or which did she think I was?

Ten minutes later

Re:

She said about one of them, 'That could be her!' About another she said, 'That's probably her!' And about the third she said, 'You'd fall in love with that one!'

Thirty seconds later

Re:

WHICH ONE WOULD YOU FALL IN LOVE WITH?????

Forty seconds later

Re:

Dear Emmi,

There's absolutely no way I'm EVER going to tell you that. Please spare yourself the effort of trying to drag it out of me. Have a nice evening. Thanks for the exciting 'game'.

I really like you, Emmi!

Yours,

Leo

Twenty-five seconds later

Re:

The blonde with the large breasts, right?

Fifty seconds later

Re:

Forget it, Emmi dear!

One minute later

Re:

An evasive answer is an answer nonetheless. The blonde with the large breasts it is, then!

The following evening

Subject: A bad day

Dear Leo,

Did you have a good day today? Mine was awful. Good evening, goodnight.

Emmi

(By the way, when you think of Emmi now, which Emmi comes to mind? I hope you *are* still thinking of Emmi!)

Three and a half hours later

Re:

When I think of Emmi, I don't think of any of the three Emmis described by my sister, but of the fourth one, my one. And yes, of course I'm still thinking about Emmi. Why didn't you have a good day? What was so awful about it? Goodnight, good morning.

Yours,

Leo

The following day

Subject: A good day!

Good morning. So you see, dear Leo, this is how a good day begins for me! I open my inbox and find a message from Leo Leike. Yesterday: bad day. No e-mail from Leo. Not one. Not a single one. Not even a hint of one. What promise does a day like that hold? Leo, I need to tell you something: I think we should stop. I'm beginning to get addicted to you. I can't spend my entire day waiting for e-mails from a man who turns his back on me when he meets me, who doesn't want to get to know me, who only wants me to e-mail him, who uses my words to construct a woman of his own making, because the presence of real women probably pushes him way beyond his comfort level. I can't go on like this. It's unrewarding. Do you understand me, Leo?

Two hours later

Re:

O.K., I understand you. But I've got four questions, which I shall set out strictly in accordance with the Rothner formula:

1) Do you want to get to know me in person?
2) Why?
3) Where will it lead?
4) Should your husband know about it?

Half an hour later

Re:

Re: 1) Do I want to get to know you in person? Of course I do. Personally is preferable to impersonally, don't you think?

Re: 2) Why? I'll only know the answer to that when we've got to know each other.

Re: 3) Where will it lead? It will lead to wherever it leads. And if it didn't lead there, then it shouldn't. So it will only lead to where it should lead.

Re: 4) Should my husband know about it? I'll only know the answer to that when I know where it's leading.

Five minutes later

Re:

So would you cheat on your husband?

One minute later

Re:

That's not what I said.

Forty seconds later

Re:

I'm inferring it.

Thirty-five seconds later

Re:

Be careful that you don't infer too much.

Two minutes later

Re:

What is it your husband can't give you?

Fifteen seconds later

Re:

Nothing. Nothing whatsoever. What gives you the impression there's something he can't give me?

Fifty seconds later

Re:

I'm inferring it.

Thirty seconds later

Re:

From what are you inferring it? (You're beginning to get on my nerves with your language psychologist's inference.)

Ten minutes later

Re:

I'm inferring it from the way you lead me to understand that you want something from me. You won't be able to say what it is until we've met. But there's no doubt that you *do* want something from me. Or put another way: you're looking for something. Let's call it adventure. Those who go looking for adventure never find it. Am I right?

An hour and a half later

Re:

You're right, I am looking for something. I desperately need a priest to explain to me the definition of cheating on your husband. Or at least what a priest might imagine it to be, a priest who has never cheated, not only because he doesn't have a woman to cheat with, but also because he doesn't have a wife to cheat on, except for the Virgin Mary herself. This isn't *The Thorn Birds*, Leo! I'm not looking for 'adventure' with you. I want to see who you are, that's all. Just once I want to look my e-mail buddy in the eye. If that's what you call 'cheating', then I admit that I might well be a cheat.

Twenty minutes later
Re:

But just to be sure, you wouldn't tell your husband anything.

Fifteen minutes later
Re:

Leo, I don't like it when you come over all priggish! You're welcome to go on like that when it concerns your own affairs, but not when it comes to mine. Being happily married doesn't mean that you have to deliver a daily report of all the people you meet. If I did that, I'd bore Bernhard to tears.

Two minutes later

Re:

So you'd say nothing to your Bernhard about our meeting because you're afraid it would bore him to tears?

Three minutes later

Re:

Oh, the way you write 'your Bernhard', Leo! I can't help it that my husband has a name. But that doesn't mean that he belongs to me, or that he's glued to my side 24/7 with me endlessly cooing 'My Bernhard!' and my hands all over him. I don't think you have the faintest idea about marriage,

Leo.

Five minutes later

Re:

I've not said a word about marriage, Emmi. And you still haven't answered my last question. But how did you put it recently? An evasive answer is an answer nonetheless.

Ten minutes later

Re:

Dear Leo,

Let's draw a line under this. You're the one who owes *me* an answer to my crucial question, which I'm happy to repeat for you: Do you want to meet me? If the answer's yes, then let's do it! If the answer's no, then please tell me what all this is about, how should it carry on? Or rather, should it carry on at all?

Twenty minutes later

Re:

Why can't we just carry on writing to each other?

Two minutes later

Re:

I don't get it: he just doesn't want to get to know me! You're such a fuddy-duddy, Leo. Maybe I'm the blonde with the large breasts!!!

Thirty seconds later
Re:
So?

Twenty seconds later
Re:
You could ogle them.

Thirty-five seconds later
Re:
And you'd like that, would you?

Twenty-five seconds later
Re:
Not me, you! All men like it, especially the ones who don't admit it.

Fifty seconds later
Re:
I much prefer these sorts of conversations.

Thirty seconds later

Re:

Aha! So you're a repressed sex-chat addict after all.

Three minutes later

Re:

That was a good one to end on, Emmi. Sorry, I've got to go out now. I hope you have a nice evening.

Four minutes later

Re:

Twenty-eight e-mails between us today, Leo. And where have they got us? Nowhere. What's your mantra? — detachment. What's *your* parting shot? — you hope that I 'have a nice evening'. That's in 'Merry Christmas and a Happy New Year from Emmi Rothner' territory. To sum up, after a hundred e-mails and a professionally executed meeting-without-actually-meeting, we're not a millimetre closer. The only thing sustaining our 'inner nonacquaintance' is the staggering effort we devote to it. Leo. Leo. Leo. What a shame, what a terrible shame.

One minute later

Re:

If a day goes by when I don't e-mail you, you complain. And if I send you fourteen e-mails in five hours, you still complain. I don't seem to be able to do right by you at the moment, Emmi.

Twenty seconds later

Re:

Not bye-mail at any rate!!! I hope you have a nice evening, Mr Leike.

Four days later

Subject: (no subject)

Peekaboo!

BW,

Emmi

The following day

Subject: (no subject)

If that's what you call tactics, Leo, it's pretty rubbish I must say! You can like me as much as you want, but I'm not writing to you any more. See ya.

Five days later

Subject: (no subject)

You haven't been cut off, have you? I'm beginning to get worried. At least write 'baa-aa' or something.

Three minutes later

Re:

O.K., Emmi, let's meet, I don't care. Do you still want to? When? Today? Tomorrow? Day after tomorrow?

Fifteen minutes later

Re:

Hark at him, back from the dead! — And now all of a sudden he seems to be in a hurry to meet me. Well, maybe I will. But first you're going to have to explain to me why you haven't been in touch for a week and a half. And it had better be good!!

Ten minutes later

Re:

My mother died. Is that good enough?

Twenty seconds later

Re:

Shit. Are you being serious? How?

Three minutes later

Re:

On balance, bad luck. In the hospital they called it a 'malignant tumour'. Fortunately it all happened pretty quickly. She wasn't in pain for long.

One minute later

Re:

Were you with her when she died?

Three minutes later

Re:

Almost. I was in the waiting room with my sister. The doctors said it wouldn't be a good time to see her. But I wonder when there could ever have been a better time.

Five minutes later

Re:

Were you close? (I'm sorry, Leo, people always seem to ask the same questions.)

Four minutes later

Re:

A week ago I'd have said no, we weren't close at all. Today, though, I'm wondering what it is that's eating away inside me, if not a 'closeness'. But I don't want to bore you with my family history, Emmi.

Six minutes later

Re:

You're not boring me at all, Leo. Do you want to meet up to talk about it? I might be just the right person in the circumstances. I'm on the very periphery of your life — and yet I'm also quite close to you. Just for once let's do away with all the formalities — let's meet like good old friends.

Ten minutes later

Re:

O.K., let's. Thank you, Emmi! Shall we meet this evening? But I should warn you, my sense of humour's bottoming out again.

Three minutes later

Re:

Dear, dear Leo,

I can't this evening. How about tomorrow, around 7? At some café in the centre?

Eight minutes later

Re:

The funeral's tomorrow. But 7 p.m. should be fine. I'll send you an e-mail before 5. Then we'll arrange exactly where to meet. O.K.?

Ten minutes later

Re:

O.K., that sounds good. I'd love to be able to say something that might comfort you. But it might sound a bit like my 'Merry Christmas and a Happy New Year', so I'd better not. I'm thinking of you. I can imagine how you're feeling. I don't even dare to wish you 'goodnight', because I'm sure tonight won't be a good one for you. But I'll be able to offer you some support tomorrow evening.

See you soon!

Emmi (and despite the awful circumstances, I'm looking forward to seeing you!)

Five minutes later

Re:

I'm looking forward to it, too!

Leo

The next day

Subject: Sorry

Dear Emmi,

I'm afraid I've got to cry off this evening. I'll tell you why tomorrow. Please don't be angry. And thanks for your support. I really appreciate it.

Best wishes,

Leo

No problem.

Emmi

Dear Emmi,

I spent yesterday evening with Marlene, my ex-girlfriend. She was at the funeral too. She really liked my mother, and vice-versa. It was important for me to talk everything through with her. She's like a key; she can open doors to my awkward family history. She also got through to my mother in a way that I never could. Marlene was in a bit of a state yesterday. It was *me* who had to console *her*. But that was O.K. by me. I can't stand people feeling sorry for me. I prefer to feel sorry for someone else. (For myself too sometimes, but I'll keep that private.) I hope you're not angry with me for standing you up. I also thought: Leo, why do you have to drag in a woman who's got nothing to do with your past? And then I didn't want you to see me as I am just now. I want you to meet me when I'm in better shape. I hope you understand, Emmi.

And thank you once again for your support. That was a major show of trust.

Love,

Leo

Three hours later

Re:

That's O.K.

BW,

Emmi

Five minutes later

Re:

No, nothing's O.K. when you write, 'That's O.K.'! What is it, Emmi? Have I seriously offended you by cancelling? Does it feel as if I've used you (and that now you're pretty redundant)?

Two and a half hours later

Re:

No, not at all, Leo. I'm just really busy, that's why I kept it short.

110

Eight minutes later
Re:

I don't believe you. I know you, Emmi. In some respects, at least. It's odd, but the very idea that I might have offended you is giving me a bad conscience, even though you know more than anyone that you'd have no right to be offended.

Four minutes later
Re:

Don't beat about the bush, dear Leo: have you got something going with Marlene again? Did you manage to console her, at least?

Eight minutes later
Re:

Oh, so that's it! Yes, of course. Leo Leike dares to meet up with his ex-girlfriend after his mother's funeral. Emmi Rothner, who is usually at great pains to make Mr Leike out to be a professor of moral theology, suddenly gets a whiff of moral degeneracy. Let me throw something else into the mix, Emmi dear. I'll admit to you that six hours after having buried my mother I came within a hair's breadth of sleeping with my

111

ex-girlfriend. I hope you're suitably shocked!
Goodnight.

Three minutes later
Re:

Please explain to me how you can come
'within a hair's breadth' of sleeping with
someone. And if you came 'within a hair's
breadth', why didn't you just get on and do
it? That's so typically male. You probably
imagined you would be able to 'console' your
stricken ex-girlfriend into bed. But at the last
minute she must have realized and whispered
in your ear 'No, Leo, it would be all wrong
for us just now. It would destroy all the trust
that we've rebuilt this evening.' And you
thought to yourself: Damn shame, I was
within a hair's breadth . . .

Fifteen minutes later
Re:

Do you know what, dear Emmi? I can hardly
believe the brazenness and tenacity with
which you're trying to draw explanations
from me about private matters that don't
concern you one iota. Or your ability to
choose the most unfortunate moment to utter

112

such tasteless comments, whose sole aim must be to reduce other people to the one thing that's always at the front of your mind: sex, sex, sex. I'm starting to wonder why you're like that.

Eight minutes later

Re:

Dear Leo,

With the greatest respect for your loss, who's the one who boasted that he'd come 'within a hair's breadth' of sleeping with someone? Me or you? I'm sorry, Leo, I can picture the scene vividly. In the past I've experienced situations like that only too often myself, and I've got lots of friends who still experience them all the time — and suffer as a result. If with you and Marlene it was completely different, then you'll have to forgive me. But a man with your sensitivities should know that a woman with my sensitivities would feel sorely rejected after a last-minute ex-girlfriend-motivated cancellation like that. Yes indeed, Leo, I feel I've been horribly rejected by you. I'm not just anybody, not even to you.

Yours respectfully,

Emmi

Subject: Emmi

No, Emmi, you're not just anybody. If there's anyone who isn't just anybody then it's you. Not to me, at any rate. You're like a second voice inside me, accompanying me through the day. You've turned my inner monologue into a dialogue. You enrich my emotional life. You question, insist, parody, you engage me in conflict. I'm so grateful to you for your wit, your charm, for your spirit, even for your tastelessness.

But Emmi, you mustn't try to become my conscience! To go back to one of your favourite subjects, it should be irrelevant to you when, how, with whom, and how often I have sex. After all, I don't ask you how things are in bed with you and your Bernhard. To be honest, I'm not the slightest bit interested. It's not that I never have erotic thoughts when I think about you. But I'm keeping them well away from you; I want to spare you these thoughts. They're inside me and that's where they'll remain. We mustn't start intruding into each other's private life. It won't get us anywhere.

Exchanging a few seemingly irrelevant words with you about my mother's death has done me the world of good, Emmi. That second voice was there again, asking 'my' missing questions, finding 'my' answers, always breaching and overcoming my loneliness. All of a sudden I had this pressing desire to get closer to you, to have you right beside me. And if you'd had time that evening it would have happened. Everything would now be different between us. All the secrets would be gone, all the puzzles solved. We'd no sooner have met than I'd have offloaded a heavy rucksack full of my family burdens, and both of us would have sunk to our knees. No more magic, no more illusions. We'd have talked and talked and talked until we were all talked out. And what then? Nothing but disenchantment. How do you handle the immediacy of a meeting if you've never had any practice? How would we have looked at each other? What would we have seen in each other? How would we be writing to each other now? What would we write? Would we still be writing to each other? Emmi, I'm just afraid of losing my 'second voice', the Emmi voice. I want to keep it. I want to treat it with care. I can't live without it.

Yours,

Leo

Three hours later

Re:

Just to come back to one of my favourite subjects: I'm sorry to say that yes, IT DOES MATTER TO ME WHEN, HOW, WITH WHOM, AND HOW OFTEN YOU HAVE SEX! If I am indeed somebody's chosen 'second voice', then I should also have the right to judge (if that's what we're talking about) whether it's appropriate when, how, with whom and how often that person has sex. (At this point I should admit that I haven't until now been especially interested in the 'how' bit, dear Leo. But we can catch up on that another time.) Now I'm going to leave you alone with your own voice. More tomorrow.

Kiss kiss,

Emmi

An hour and a half later

Re:

May I for once be cynical too, my dearest Emmi? Let's say the 'hairy beast' in Café Huber had been me. Would it then have mattered when, how, with whom, and how often I have sex? Or, to put it another way, does it only matter to you when, how . . . and so on, because in your e-mails you're in search of an ideal man, and it can't be irrelevant — in spite of your marital bliss with Bernhard — when, how . . . and so on? This would confirm my theory that each of us is the fantasy voice of the other. Is this not wonderful and precious enough to leave it as it is?

The following day

Subject: First answer

Dear Leo,

Do you know what I really can't stand about you? — the words you use when you talk about my husband. 'In spite of your marital bliss with Bernhard' — tell me, please, what do you mean by that crap? 'Marital bliss' sounds like: 'Performing one's conjugal duty by having sexual intercourse with one's partner.' I'm sure you intended it to sound like that too! Or how about: 'A regular consummation of sexual intercourse, blessed by marriage, with a corresponding exchange of bodily fluids.' My dear Leo, you're mocking my marriage! I can be extremely sensitive on the subject, so please desist!

Forty-five minutes later

Re:

Emmi, you can't stop talking about sex. It's pathological!

One hour later

Re:

I haven't even *started* talking about sex, my friend. A few of the remarks you made yesterday are worth picking up on, for example the thing about the 'erotic thoughts' where you use a double negative to say that it's not that you never have erotic thoughts about me. Typical Leo! Anyone else would have said: 'Emmi, sometimes I have erotic thoughts about you!' But Leo Leike says: 'Emmi, it's not that I never have erotic thoughts when I think about you.' And then you wonder why I can't stop talking about sex. It's not me who's pathological — you're the one who's so 'original' with your sex talk, my dear Leo! In short, I don't buy your lofty meditations on sex. And what is our saintly Leo doing with his double-negative erotic thoughts? I quote: 'I'm keeping them well away from you; I want to spare you these thoughts.' But doesn't he want to disclose them? Now Emmi's wondering what these unspeakable thoughts might be. Maybe he'll tell me a little more about them?

Twenty minutes later

Re:

Oh yes, and another thing, Mr Leo. Yesterday you wrote: 'We must not start intruding into each other's private life.' I've got something to tell you: what we're doing here, the things we're talking about, they already belong to our private lives. They're private and nothing but, starting with our very first e-mails and steadily escalating until today. We don't write about our jobs, we don't say what our interests are, or our hobbies. We behave as if there's no such thing as culture, we completely ignore politics, and by and large we get by without even mentioning the weather. The only thing we do, the thing that makes us forget everything else, is to intrude into each other's private life; I enter yours, and you enter mine. We could hardly have been more intrusive into each other's private life. You should start facing the fact that you're intimately acquainted with my private life, if not the part of it that you call my favourite subject. I might even say that the situation couldn't be more different.

Have a nice evening,
Emmi

An hour and a half later
Re:

Dear Emmi,

Do you know what I really can't stand about *you*? Your continual 'Mr Leo', 'Maestro Leo', 'Professor Leo', 'Mr Language Psychologist', 'professor of moral theology'. Do me a favour. Leave it at 'Leo'. Your sarcastic messages will be just as acerbic and to the point.

Thanks for your understanding!
Leo

Ten minutes later
Re:

Yuck! I don't like you today!

One minute later
Re:

I don't like me either.

Thirty seconds later

Re:

That was very sweet, I have to admit.

Twenty seconds later

Re:

Thank you.

Fifteen seconds later

Re:

My pleasure.

A minute and a half later

Re:

Are you in bed yet?

Three minutes later

Re:

I hardly ever go to bed before you. Night night!

Thirty seconds later
Re:
Goodnight.

Forty seconds later
Re:
Are you thinking about your mother a lot? I wish I could help share your sadness.

Thirty seconds later
Re:
You just have, dear Emmi.
Goodnight.

4

Three days later

Subject: Break over!

Dear Emmi,

We've now had a three-day break from e-mailing. I think we can slowly resume our correspondence. I hope you have a good day at work. I'm thinking of you a lot, in the mornings, in the afternoons, in the evenings, at night, in the periods in-between and just before and after — and also during.

Love,

Leo

Ten minutes later

Re:

M (Ma-Mae-Maes-Maest . . .) Dear Leo,

YOU might have had a break from e-mailing, but I haven't! I've been hard at work watching you take your e-mail break. And I've been waiting for you to finish your e-mail break. I've been getting quite impatient. But it's been worth it. Here you are again, and you're thinking of me. That's nice. Are you well? Do you have the time and the inclination for a glass of wine with me later on this evening? Not together, of course. I mean you and your fantasy Emmi. And me and my virtual Leo. And we can write to each other a bit while we're at it. Do you fancy it?

Eight minutes later

Re:

Yes, Emmi, let's do that. Is your B (Be, Ber, Bern, Bernh), is your husband out in the evenings?

Three minutes later

Re:

You just love asking me questions like that, don't you? It always sounds a bit like you want to punish me for being happily married. No, Bernhard is at home in the evenings. He'll either be in his study preparing work for tomorrow or he'll be sitting on his sofa reading. Or he'll be asleep in his bed. He's usually asleep by midnight. Is that a good enough answer?

Six minutes later

Re:

Yes, perfectly adequate, thank you! Whenever you talk about your husband, Emmi, it always sounds as if you want to prove that you can lead separate and independent lives, even if, or although, or precisely because, you're married. You don't write 'in the study', but 'in *his* study'. He doesn't sit 'on our sofa', but 'on *his* sofa'. He doesn't even lie 'in our bed', but 'in *his* bed'.

Four minutes later

Re:

Dear Leo,

You're not going to believe this, but at our house we really do have our own studies, our own sofas and yes, even our own beds. You see, funnily enough we also have our own lives. Does that shock you?

Twenty-five seconds later

Re:

Then why do you live together?

125

Eighteen minutes later

Re:

You're so sweet, Leo! You're as naïve as a twenty-year-old. We don't pin 'Keep Out' signs to our study doors, our sofas are not for 'authorized personnel only'. Our beds don't carry the warning 'Beware — it bites!' Each of us has our own domain, but we're also very welcome to enter each other's. As you and I put it only recently, we're welcome to 'intrude into each other's private life'. So now you've found out a bit more about my marriage.

Thirty seconds later

Re:

And how old are the children?

Thirty-five minutes later

Re:

Fiona is sixteen, Jonas eleven. And 'my Bernhard' is considerably older than I am. So, my dear Leo, that brings us to the end of your lesson about my family. If it's all the same to you, I'd rather leave the children out of our exchanges. A few months ago you said you found chatting to me was like a kind of 'Marlene therapy'. (Of course I don't know whether that's still the case — perhaps you could let me know one of these days!) For me writing to you and reading your e-mails is like non-family time. It's a little island outside my daily experience, a tiny island which I'd much rather inhabit with you alone, if you don't mind.

Five minutes later

Re:

That's fine, Emmi. Sometimes I'm just niggled by a curiosity to know what you're like outside of our fuzzy little island, what your grounded life on the mainland is like, in the secure harbour of your marriage. (Forgive me, it just worked so well.) But I'm all island again now. So when are we going to drink our glass of wine? Midnight too late for you?

Two minutes later

Re:

Midnight would be perfect! I look forward to our rendezvous.

Twenty seconds later

Re:

Me too. Till then.

Midnight

Subject: (no subject)

Dear Emmi,

Leo here. Here's to a heavenly midnight, *à deux*, just for the two of us. May I embrace you, Emmi? May I kiss you? I will kiss you. Right, let's drink. What are you drinking? I'm drinking Sauvignon Visconti, Colli Orientali del Friuli, 2003. And what are you drinking? Reply immediately, Emmi, immediately, O.K.? What's Emmi drinking? I'm drinking white wine.

One minute later

Re:

Doesn't sound like your first glass!!!

Eight minutes later

Re:

Oh look, Emmi's writing again. Emmi. Emmi. Emmi. I'm a little drunk, but only a little. I've been drinking all evening and waiting for midnight, until Emmi comes to visit me. Yes, you're right. It's not my first bottle. I'm longing for my Emmi. Do you fancy coming over here? We can turn the lights off. We don't have to see each other. I just want to feel you, Emmi. I'll close my eyes. It's pointless with Marlene. We're draining the life-blood from each other. We don't love each other. She thinks we do, but we don't, it isn't love, it's just enslavement, just possession. Marlene doesn't want to let me go, and I, well, I can't hold on to her. I'm a bit drunk. Not very. Will you come over, Emmi? Shall we kiss? My sister says you're very beautiful, Emmi, whoever you are. Have you ever kissed a stranger? I'm going to have another swig of the Friuli now. I'll drink to us both. I'm a bit drunk already. But not very. And now it's your turn again. Write to me, Emmi. Writing is like kissing, but without lips. Writing is kissing with the mind. Emmi, Emmi, Emmi.

Four minutes later

Re:

Ah well, I suppose I imagined our first midnight date would be a bit different. Leo pissed as a fart!! But it does have a certain charm. Do you know what? I'll make it short — the words are probably swimming at this stage anyway. But if you're in the mood, if you can manage it, why don't you tell me a bit more about your home life. Please don't write anything that you might regret tomorrow morning, when you wake from your delirium. I'm going to drink a glass of red from the Rhone valley, a 1997. Here's to you! But I'd advise you to switch to water. Or make yourself a strong coffee.

Fifty minutes later

Re:

You're so harsh, Emmi. Don't be so harsh. I don't want coffee. I want Emmi. Come over to my place. Let's drink another small glass of wine. We could wear blindfolds, like in the film. I don't know what the film's called, I'll have to think about it. I'd really love to kiss you. I don't care what you look like. I've fallen in love with your words. Write what you want. Feel free to be harsh. I love it all. You see, deep down you're not harsh really. But you force yourself to be, you just want to make out you're stronger than you are. Marlene doesn't touch booze. Marlene is a very sober woman, yet fascinating. That's what everybody who knows her says. She got together with a pilot, from Spain. But it's all over now. She says there's only one man for her and that's me. That's a lie, you know. She can't have me any more. It really hurts when you split up. I don't want to split up from Marlene again. My mother liked her, but she's dead, she was unlucky. It's very different from how I thought it would be. Part of me has died with her. I've only been aware of it since that part of me died. My mother wasn't that interested in me, just in my little sister. And my father emigrated to Canada and took my older brother with him. I fell somewhere in-between. I was ignored. I was a quiet child. I can show you photos. Do you want to see photos? I was always Buster Keaton at carnival time. I like silent, sad, funny heroes who can pull faces. Come over, let's drink another glass to us and look through carnival photos. Shame you're married. No, it's a good thing you're married. Would you cheat on your husband, Emmi? Don't do it. It hurts so terribly to be cheated on. I'm already a little drunk, but my head's still clear. Marlene cheated on me once. I mean, once that I know of. You take one look at Marlene and you know that she'll cheat on you. I'm putting that all behind me now, Emmi. Here's a kiss. And another kiss. And another kiss.

And another. Whoever you are. I long to be close. I don't want to think about my mother. I don't want to think about Marlene. I want to kiss Emmi. Excuse me, I'm a bit drunk. It's all behind me now. I'm off to bed. Goodnight kiss. Shame you're married. I think we'd be good together. Emmi. Emmi. Emmi. I like writing Emmi. Left middle finger once, right index finger twice and, two rows above that, right middle finger. E M M I. I could write Emmi a thousand times. Writing Emmi is kissing Emmi. Let's go to bed, Emmi.

The next morning
Subject: Hi
Hi Leo,
How's your head?
Lots of love from Emmi

Two and a half hours later
Subject: (no subject)
Are you still wondering how to explain to yourself and, more to the point, how to explain to *me* last night's e-mails? You don't have to, Leo. I liked all those things you came out with; I really liked them, in fact. You should get drunk more often, you become a

much more emotional person: very open and forthright, tender, even bordering on ardent and passionate. This unbridled side suits you! I'm honoured that you wanted to kiss me so often! So please write to me. I badly need to know what you think about all this. You always try to rein yourself in when you're sober, quite different from the Leo who's unleashed when he's a bit drunk. I hope you didn't throw up.

Three hours later

Subject: (no subject)

Leo???? Why aren't you writing back! It's not fair, and it's a real turn off. It smacks of a man who in the morning is not willing to stand by what he whispered into a woman's ear the night before, when he was drunk on love. It smacks of a pretty typical, pretty average, pretty dull man. But it doesn't smack of Leo. So will you please write to me!!!!

Five hours later

Re:

Dear Emmi,

It's now ten o'clock. Do you want to come

over to my place? I'll pay the taxi fare. (I live on the edge of town.)

Leo

Almost two hours later

Re:

Whoops! Dear Leo, it's now 23.43. Are you still dreaming, or are you asleep? If not, I've got a few questions for you:

1) Did you really want me to come over?
2) Do you still want me to come over?
3) Might you be 'a bit drunk' again?
4) If I came over to your place, what do you think you and I might do?

Five minutes later

Re:

Dear Emmi,

1) Yes
2) Yes
3) No
4) We'll see what happens.

Three minutes later

Re:

Dear Leo,

1) O.K.
2) Right
3) Good
4) We'll see what happens? Whatever happens is always what people want to happen. So what do you want to happen?

Fifty seconds later

Re:

I really don't know, Emmi. But I think we'll know the moment we meet.

Two minutes later

Re:

And what if nothing happens? Then we'll just stand there like idiots, shrugging our shoulders, and one of us will say to the other: 'Really sorry, for some reason nothing's happening.' And then what?

One minute later

Re:

That's a risk we'll have to take. So do come over, Emmi! Be brave! Let's both be brave! Let's trust in each other!

Twenty-five minutes later

Re:

Dear Leo,

I find your urgency strange, and it's beginning to get on my nerves. It's not your usual style. I have a hunch that you know exactly what might happen. You're probably still feeling the effects of last night. Are you still on a bit of a high? You're looking for intimacy. You want to forget Marlene, or rather, you want to make her forgotten. And you've read enough books on how this works, you've seen plenty of films, last tangos with Marlon Brandos and so forth. I know those scenes, Leo: he sees her for the first time, preferably in semi-darkness, so that everything looks beautiful even if it isn't. And then not another word is spoken, and the only sound is of clothes dropping to the ground. They fall on each other as if they're about to die of starvation, they stop at nothing, rolling around for hours from one end of some

136

designer apartment to the other. End of scene. In the next shot he's lying on his back with a self-satisfied smile playing across his lips. His eyes wander lasciviously across the ceiling, as if he even wants to have it off with that too. She lies there with her head on his chest, satiated like some doe after a herd of rutting stags has passed through. One of them might be having a cigarette, exhaling smoke through his or her nose. And then there'll be a subtle fade-out. But what happens after that? That's what most interests me. What happens after that???

That's not the way it's going to happen, Leo. Just for once you've been behaving like a stereotypical male. We could have got round all this, of course. That blindfold fantasy you let slip yesterday when you were drunk — we wouldn't even have to see each other. You open the door to me with a blindfold on, and we fall into each other's arms. We have sex blindfold. We say goodbye to each other blindfold. And tomorrow you'd write me more sanctimonious e-mails about fidelity and I'd write you bolshie e-mails back, like I always do. And if our night together was good, we'd do it again, uncoupled from our other lives, entirely independent of our correspondence. Sex with the minimum attachment possible. We've got nothing to lose, nothing would be jeopardized. You'd have your 'intimacy', I'd have my little extra-marital adventure. It's an exciting prospect, I must say. But let's face it, it's a bit of a male fantasy, dear Leo, and we should run a mile from it. Or to spell it out, you can forget it with me! (And I say that very gently, I promise!)

Fifteen minutes later

Re:

What if I'd only wanted to show you a few photos of me when I was a child? What if I'd only wanted to drink a whisky or a vodka sour with you — to our health and our groundbreaking achievement of having met at last? What if I'd only wanted to hear your voice? And what if I'd only wanted to breathe in the scent of your hair and skin?

Nine minutes later

Re:

Leo, Leo, Leo, sometimes it sounds as if you're the woman in this set-up, and I'm the man. But I'm convinced it's just a game we're playing at the highest level. I'm trying to think like a man so that I can understand you, I'm trying to see things from a man's perspective, I'm downloading all my mental files that relate to the way men think, including glossary — and all I get is you telling me that *I'm* the one who's obsessed with sex. I expose the classic male motives for an urgent midnight rendezvous — and you turn it all round and say they're mine. Aren't you the innocent one, Leo! What a shy romantic you are! Why can't you just admit that keeping your virtual finger pressed on my virtual doorbell at 10 o'clock at night had nothing to do with childhood photos. (Perhaps you've got a nice stamp collection, too? In which case I'd have been round like a shot . . .)

Three minutes later

Re:

Dear Emmi,

Don't ever talk about men in general when you're referring to *me* — it's a demeaning tactic, and often meant spitefully. You can't lump me together with everyone else — I'm too much of an individual — and you shouldn't use the example of other men to infer things about me. It's just such an insult!

Eighteen minutes later

Re:

O.K., O.K., I'm sorry! But look how you've just cunningly dodged explaining your real motive for wanting to see me so urgently in the middle of the night. In your hungover infatuation and need for a shag, Leo, there's no disgrace in trying to pull the old blindfold trick with Emmi, whom you don't even know (although apparently she's not so bad looking). In fact I'm extremely flattered, and you haven't sunk so much as a millimetre in my estimation. It's 1.30 in the morning, by the way, time I thought about going to bed. Thanks again for your thrilling offer. Very daring of you. I like it when you're spontaneous. And I also like it when you drunkenly shower me with kisses. Night night, Leo, with a kiss from me too.

Five minutes later

Re:

I wouldn't try to pull a fast one on anyone, ever.

Goodnight.

Twelve minutes later

Re:

Just two more things, Leo. I can't sleep anyway. If I really had come over to your place, you don't think I'd have made you pay for the taxi, do you?

And if I really had come over to your place, which of the three Emmis on your sister's list would you have wanted? Bubbly Ur-Emmi? Busty Blonde-Emmi? Or shy Surprise-Emmi? Because I'm sure you already know that your Fantasy-Emmi would have disappeared for good the moment we met.

One day later

Subject: I.T. issues?

Leo? Your turn!

Three days later

Subject: Break in correspondence

Emmi,

I'm just writing to let you know that it's not that I'm stopping our correspondence for good. The moment I know WHAT to write, I'll write it. I'm in the process of assembling the schizophrenic fragments I've been broken up

141

into over the past few days. I'll write just as soon as I've put all the pieces back together again.

You haunt me constantly, Emmi. I miss you. I'm longing for you. I read your e-mails over and over again, every day.

Yours,

Leo

Four days later

Subject: Confession

Hello Mr Leike,

Do you have a guilty conscience? Have you got a confession to make? Is there something I should know? If so, I think I know what that thing is. I've found something dreadful in my inbox. Do you know what I'm talking about? Feel free to unburden yourself!!!

Best wishes,

Emmi Rothner

Three and a half hours later

Re:

What's wrong with you, Emmi? What's that cryptic e-mail supposed to mean? Are you concocting some sort of conspiracy theory? Whatever it is, I've got no idea what you're talking about. What dreadful thing did you find your inbox? Please be a bit clearer! And don't be so bloody formal just because you're suspicious!

Love,

Leo

Half an hour later

Re:

Oh most esteemed language psychologist, if it turns out that my suspicions are well founded, I'll detest you for the rest of my life! You'd better come out with it right now.

Twenty-five minutes later

Re:

Whatever it is that's put you in this mood, dear Emmi, your language frightens me. I don't want to be a victim of your speculative blind hatred, based as it is on confused thoughts and ludicrous associations in a brain eaten away by mistrust. Either give it to me straight or reassure me you like me! Because right now I'm furious.

Leo

143

The next day

Subject: Confession II

On Sunday I met up with a friend of mine. I told her about you, Leo. 'What does he do for a living?' she asked me. 'He's a language psychologist — he works at the university,' I replied. Language psychology. Sonja was amazed. 'What does he do there?' she then asked. And I said: 'I don't know exactly. We don't talk about our work, just about ourselves.' And then I remembered. At the beginning he mentioned something about doing a study on the language of e-mails. That's what he was working on at the time. But then there was no more mention of it. In a flash Sonja's expression darkened and she literally said: 'Be careful, Emmi, he may just be analyzing you!' I was so shocked. The first thing I did when I got home was to sit down and start reading through our old e-mails. And I found the following paragraph from you from 20 February: 'We're currently working on a study that's looking at the influence of e-mail on our linguistic behaviour and — the much more interesting part of the project — e-mail as a medium for conveying our emotions. This is why I tend to talk shop, but in future I promise to restrain myself.'

So, my dear Leo, maybe now you understand why I feel the way I do? LEO, ARE YOU ANALYZING ME? ARE YOU JUST TEST-ING ME AS A MEDIUM FOR CONVEYING EMOTIONS? AM I NOTHING MORE THAN THE CONTENT OF A COLD PHD THESIS OR SOME OTHER GHASTLY LANGUAGE EXPERIMENT?

Forty minutes later

Re:

If I were you I'd ask Bernhard what he thinks about it, because I've had enough of you. Besides, any means of conveyance would collapse under the weight of your emotional baggage.

Leo

Five minutes later

Re:

You can go on the counter-attack if you want, but don't think my concerns about being exploited by a language psychologist have gone away. So please be straight with me. You owe me that much, Leo.

Three days later

Subject: Leo!

Dear Leo,

The last three days have been horrible. On the one hand I've been terrified — yes, it was a real panic attack — that you've been using me all along for some study, and on the other I'm plagued by the awful misgiving that I might have done you an injustice. Perhaps my rash accusations have destroyed something between us. I've no idea what would be worse: to have been 'betrayed' by you, or, in an attack of blind suspicion, to have bulldozed the refuge of our mutual trust which we've so lovingly and carefully built up.

Dear Leo, please try to put yourself in my shoes. I must confess I haven't had such an intense emotional exchange with anyone for a long time. I'd never have believed that this was possible. In my e-mails to you I can be the real Emmi, in a way that I can't be at any other time. In what we call 'real life' — if you want to be successful, if you want to get on in the long term — you always have to come to some kind of compromise with your own emotions: I can't overreact *now*! I have to accept *this*! I have to ignore *that*! — You're forever having to tailor your emotions to the circumstances, you go easy on the people you love, you slip into your hundred little daily roles, you juggle, you balance, you weigh things up so as not to jeopardize the entire structure, because you yourself have a stake in it.

But with you, dear Leo, I'm not afraid to be spontaneous, or true to my inner self. I don't need to think about what I can tell you and what I can't. I just witter on blithely. It does me so much good!!! And that's all down to you, Leo. That's why you've become so essential to me: you take me just as I am. Sometimes you rein me in, sometimes you ignore things, sometimes you take things the wrong way. But your patience, the fact that you stick with me, shows me that I can be who I am. And, if you'll allow me to blow my own trumpet a little, I'm much more gentle than my e-mails might lead you to believe. Which means that someone out there likes the Emmi who lets herself go, who couldn't care less about making a good impression, who insists on drawing attention to her shortcomings — yes, Leo, I'm jealous, yes, I'm untrusting, I'm a bit neurotic, and I don't have a particularly high opinion of the opposite sex, nor even of my own — now I'm losing the thread. Where was I? — But someone out there likes the Emmi who makes no effort to be a good person, who plays up weaknesses that would otherwise be suppressed. He's interested in Emmi as she really is; he likes her precisely because she's aware that there's so much of herself she cannot reveal to others, this bundle of moods, this harbour of self-doubt, this jumble of contradictions.

But it's not just about me, Leo. I think about you all the time. You've occupied a few square millimetres of my cerebrum (or maybe it's the cerebellum, or pituitary gland, I've got no idea where I base my thoughts about someone like you.) You've effectively set up camp there. I don't know if you're the same person as the man who writes to me. But even if you're only a part of that man, you're still very special. Your lines to me and my interpretation of them yield up the kind of man I now suddenly realize does actually exist. You've always written about your 'fantasy Emmi'. Well maybe I'm less willing to content myself with a 'fantasy Leo', to have someone I'm so fond of confined to my imagination. I want him to be made of flesh and blood and stuff like that. And he must be up to meeting me. I know we're not at that stage yet, but I think we could come closer to a meeting through our writing. Until we get to the point where we're standing face to face. Or sitting. Or kneeling. Whatever.

Take this e-mail, for example. I find it appalling that you might be analyzing its contents word for word in order to squeeze out some kind of scientific insight, or quoting sections of it to show how or by what means emotions may be conveyed, or worse, how emotions may be aroused in others, how to write in a way which sucks someone in emotionally. I could scream in agony at the very thought!! Please tell me that our correspondence has nothing whatsoever to do with your research. And please forgive me for having thought such a thing. I'm the kind of person who has to assume the worst: it's how I build up my defences against my worst fears being realized.

That's the longest e-mail I've ever written to you, Leo. Please don't ignore it. Please come back. Don't strike camp and move on from my cerebral cortex. I need you! I . . . cherish you!

Your Emmi

P.S. I know it's *sooo* late, but I'm convinced you're still awake. I'm sure you'll check your e-mails again tonight. You don't have to answer me now. But maybe you could just write one word to let me know you've got my message? Just one, is that O.K.? Or you could make it two, or three if that's easier. Please. Please. Please. Please. Please

Two seconds later

Out of Office AutoReply

I AM AWAY AND WILL NOT BE ABLE TO CHECK E-MAILS UNTIL 18 MAY. FOR URGENT MATTERS PLEASE CONTACT THE UNIVERSITY'S INSTI-TUTE OF PSYCHOLOGY. E-MAIL: psy-uni@gr.vln.com.

One minute later

Re:

That's the pits!

5

Eight days later

Subject: Back!

Hi Emmi,

I'm back. I was in Amsterdam. With Marlene. We made another go of it. A brief attempt. After two days I was in bed with pneumonia. It was all very embarrassing; she spent five days shaking a thermometer and giving me bittersweet smiles. She was like a nurse in her thirtieth year of service who hates her job, but who tries not to blame her patients for it. Amsterdam was the opposite of what I had expected — not a fresh start, but a familiar ending, fairly routine after all these years. This time we separated with dignity. She said that if I ever needed anything she'd always help me out. What she meant was anything from the chemist. And I said, 'If you ever imagine you can't live without me, and if I convince myself that I can't live without you, I suggest we come back to Amsterdam for a few days to show ourselves just how wrong we are.'

I told Marlene about us, too. She reacted as if this was more serious than my pneumonia. I said, 'I'm obsessed with a woman on the Internet.' She said, 'How old is she? What does she look like?' I said, 'No idea. Between thirty and forty. She's either blonde, brunette or a redhead. Anyway, she's happily married.' She said, 'You're sick!'

'This woman,' I said, 'allows me to think of somebody else apart from you, Marlene, and yet have similar feelings. She winds me up, irritates me — at times I could kick her into cyberspace, but then I'm just as keen to get her back again. I need her here on earth, you see. She listens. She's clever. She's funny. And, most importantly of all, she's there for me.' 'If it helps to write to her, then write to her,' Marlene told me on the way to bed. 'And don't forget your pills,' she added.

I don't know what to do, Emmi. How can I get away from this woman? She's a block of ice, but I get hot whenever I touch her. When I walk with her through the streets of Amsterdam I get pneumonia. But when she lays her hand on my forehead at night, I begin to glow.

Right, Emmi, part two. I'm back. I've got no intention of striking camp from your cerebral cortex. I want us to keep writing to each other. And I'd like us to meet in person. By every criteria of human logic, we've missed all the obvious, right moments. We've ignored the most basic rules of being together. We're old soulmates, mutual support in our daily lives, sometimes we're even lovers. And despite this our relationship hasn't had the customary beginning: a meeting. I'm sure we'll make up for it! But I don't know how yet, without losing a part of what we are. Do you have any idea?

Right, Emmi, part three. I deliberately started my e-mail talking about Marlene. Because I'd like us to share more about our lives. I don't want to pretend there's only the two of us. I want to know how you cope with your marriage, how you manage with the children, things like that. I'd also like to know what you worry about. I'd find it a great comfort to know it's not just me who's got problems. It would help me to talk about them. It would be an honour to be taken into your strictest confidence.

Right, Emmi, part four. Please don't hate me preemptively ever again! I couldn't bear it. At the beginning of March I dropped out of the study on the influence of e-mail on our linguistic behaviour and its significance as a means of conveying emotions. The official excuse I gave was that I didn't have enough time. But in fact this subject had become too personal and I couldn't look at it scientifically any more. Does that clear things up?

Have a nice day,

Leo

P.S. Although my 'Out of office' autoreply was the correct punishment for your aggressive and suspicious note, I also did feel sorry for you. That was a really lovely, candid, honest and detailed message. Thanks for every word! Now you're a few cheeky comments in credit.

Forty-five minutes later

Re:

Did you drop out of the study because of us? That's nice, Leo, for that I love you! (Luckily you can't have a clue what I mean by that.) I've got to take Jonas to the dentist. It's a shame he's not already under general anaesthetic. There's your answer to how I manage with the kids.

Till later,

Emmi

Six hours later

Subject: (no subject)

O.K., Leo, I'm sitting in my study, Bernhard's still working, Fiona's staying over at a friend's, Jonas is asleep (minus two teeth), Wurlitzer's eating dog food (much cheaper, and Wurlitzer doesn't seem to mind, as long as there's enough of it). You know we don't have chipmunks — if we did, the cat would probably want to eat them too. I'm being stared at reproachfully by the furniture. Scenting betrayal, it threatens me: You'd better not let on how much we cost, what colour we are or what our design is! The piano's saying: Don't you dare tell him that Bernhard was your piano teacher! Don't tell him how it felt the first time you kissed, and how you made love on top of me. The bookcase is asking: Who is this Leo anyway? What's he doing here? Why do you spend so much time with him? Why do you ignore me most of the time? Why have you become so preoccupied? The C.D. player is telling me: Soon it's going to get so bad that you won't play Rachmaninov any more — don't forget how important music is to your relationship with Bernhard — instead you'll want to know what this Leo chap likes listening to. Who knows, it might be the Sugarbabes! Only the wine rack has something to say in your defence: Well, I don't have anything against Leo, the three of us get along just fine. But I hear threats from the bed: Don't lie here dreaming about being somewhere else. Don't get caught here with Leo. That's a warning!

I can't do it, Leo. I can't share this world with you. You can never become a part of it. It's impenetrable, like a fortress. It can't be conquered, it allows no-one to intrude, it resolutely keeps them out. You and I have to stay 'outside', Leo, it's our only chance. I'll lose you otherwise. You asked how I 'cope' with my marriage? Admirably, and I mean that! And Bernhard does too. He worships me. I respect and treasure him. We respect each other. He would never deceive me. I could never let him down. We would never want to hurt each other. We've built up a life together. We depend on each other. We've got music, we have theatre. We've got lots of friends in common. Fiona, she's sixteen, she's like a younger sister to me. And I really have become a kind of mother to Jonas. His mother died when he was three.

Leo, please don't force me to open my family album. Why don't we do it like this: I'll tell you about my home life if I feel like it, if I've got something on my mind, if I want to confide in a very close friend. But you can tell me about your private life any time you want, down to the very last, explosive detail. (Just don't go into anything erotic — I forbid you!)

I'm off to bed now — and I'm finally going to get a good night's sleep. I'm so glad you're back, Leo!! I need you! I have to be able to live, breathe and feel beyond my world here as well. You are my other world! And we can talk about Marlene tomorrow — I'm going to need a clear head for that. Goodnight, my love! And a goodnight kiss!

The next day

Subject: Marlene

Good morning, Leo. If you can't be with each other, and you can't be without each other, the only other option is to find someone else. You need someone else, Leo. You need to fall in love again. And that's when you'll realize what you've been missing all this time. Closeness isn't just an absence of distance, it means actively eliminating it. The thrill doesn't stem from a lack of completeness, but from constantly striving for it, and clinging on to it when you've got it. There's nothing for it, Leo, we need to find you a woman! Of course it would be naive to say 'Forget Marlene!' But you've got to, once and for all. I've got a suggestion to make. Instead of thinking about Marlene, why don't you make a conscious effort to think about me instead? Imagine you're doing everything with me that you'd like to do with Marlene. (My furniture's beginning to stare at me again.) I mean, just for the transition phase, until we've found you someone else. What kind of a woman would you like? How would you like her to look? Go on, tell me! Maybe I've got someone in mind.

Seriously now, a woman who says, 'If it helps to write to her, then write to her,' is a million miles away from what I understand by being in love. Marlene doesn't love Leo. Leo doesn't love Marlene. The passion of these two non-lovers is forged from the other's craving for love. I can't put it better than that. I have to work now.

Till soon,

Emmi, your 'virtual alternative'

Four hours later

Re:

Dear Emmi,

Greetings from your other world. I enjoy your e-mails, and I'm really grateful for them. Please tell your various pieces of furniture that I admire their attitude and respect their team spirit. I'm not going to intrude into the Rothner household; I'll restrict my dealings with Emmi to the screen. My particular compliments to the wine cabinet. Maybe one day the three of us can have another midnight rendezvous. (I promise not to drink so much beforehand.)

I'm tickled pink that you're thinking about pairing me off. What sort of women do I like? Women who look the way you write, Emmi. And I wouldn't mind getting a crack at being their real world, not just their other world. In short, women who aren't already 'happily married', holed up in a family fortress and under surveillance by their furniture. Until one of those crosses my path, I'll gladly take you up on your offer and think about you before I think of Marlene. It won't always work, but if you keep on spoiling me with e-mails I'll inch ever closer to my goal.

I hope you have a nice evening. I'm meeting up with my sister Adrienne. She'll be pleased that I've managed to split up with Marlene again. And she'll be delighted that I'm still in touch with you. All she knows is the odd excerpt from your e-mails and what I've told her about you — and she's seen the three Emmi candidates. She likes you, irrespective of which one is you. She is at one with her brother on this.

The next day

Subject: Mia!

Hi Leo, it came to me in the night. Of course, Mia! It's Mia! Leo and Mia — it sounds wonderful already! Listen to this, Leo, Mia's thirty-four and gorgeous. She's a sports teacher with long legs and a lovely figure, not an ounce of fat on her, dark complexion, black hair. There's only one drawback: she's vegetarian, but all you have to do is tell her it's tofu and she'll eat meat too. She's extremely well read, highly intelligent, enterprising, jolly, invariably in a good mood. In other words, she's a dream woman. And . . . she's single! Shall I introduce you?

An hour and a half later

Re:

Emmi, Emmi, Emmi! I know all about those long-legged Mias. My little sister introduces me to one of them practically every week. I've seen those designer clothes catalogues full of 0.0 per cent fat models *à la Mia*, each one more beautiful and longer-legged than the next. And they're all single. And do you know why, dear Emmi? Because that's how they like it! And that's how they want it to stay for a while longer.

I hate to dampen your enthusiasm, my dear other-world Emmi, but I'm not in the mood for meeting a dream Mia at the moment. I'm very happy with my life as it is. Thank you for your efforts nonetheless!

My sister sends her greetings, by the way. She says I shouldn't make the mistake of meeting you. Her exact words were, 'A meeting would be the end of your relationship. And this relationship is doing you a world of good!'

Bye,

Leo

Two hours later

Re:

O.K. Leo, our meeting can wait, I'm reconciled to that. You'll make a patient woman of me yet! I'm delighted your sister has been thinking about us. But how can she be so sure that our 'relationship' would be over if we met? And who does she think would end it: you or me?

One other thing: in your e-mail yesterday evening you referred to me as 'happily married'. Why did you put 'happily married' in inverted commas? That makes me think you wanted to make some kind of rhetorical remark, with a tiny tinge of facetiousness to it. Do you know what I mean?

Back to Mia, you've misunderstood me entirely there. She's not just some kind of eye-catching beauty from a fashion mag. Mia is a really lovely woman, and she's slipped into being single quite without wanting to. A typical case of relationship mismanagement in her younger years. When she was nineteen she met a man, an Adonis on the outside, a bundle of testosterone, a real sex machine. But on the inside he was empty, especially in the brains department. Two terrible years of waiting and hoping, and then finally he opened his mouth and the magic was gone. So she's twenty-one and immediately meets another muscle-bound guy. And she thinks: There's got to be more to this one. But there isn't, so on to the next. This develops into a classic female pattern: she thinks she needs the same kind of guy each time, to correct the 'mistakes' made first time around. But with each subsequent mistake she's drawn ever more keenly to the same type.

Mia's men have all looked identical, and not one of them was able to compensate for the shortcomings of his predecessor. On the contrary, each succeeded in confirming that his predecessor was just as hollow as he was himself. For two years she's been far too exhausted and unmotivated to meet new men. She never makes any approaches. Recently she said to me that if I ever met anyone nice, I should feel free to introduce her. But she doesn't want to have to make too much effort. If it doesn't happen of its own accord, then it won't happen at all. That's Mia for you. I'm telling you, Leo, you'll really like her.

An hour and a half later

Re:

Dear Emmi,

I'll deal with your opening questions first:

1) My sister didn't specify which of the two of us would be the first to end our 'relationship' (is it O.K. to put relationship in inverted commas?) after a meeting. She was probably thinking that our written exchanges would be incompatible with face-to-face conversation, and that would soon end the whole thing.

2) It's astonishing how much you pick up on! I didn't consciously put 'happily married' in inverted commas.
Maybe the software does it automatically. No, in all seriousness, the expression is yours and I was quoting it, because I always feel that 'happily married' is a subjective notion. I doubt, for example, that what I understand by 'happily married' is the same as you or your husband perceive it. In any case it really isn't important, is it? It was never meant to be facetious, and in future I'll leave out the inverted commas, O.K.?

And now to your friend Mia. When you next see her, by all means say you know a man who has also tried repeatedly to correct the 'mistakes' from the first time, except that he only needs, or rather needed, one woman to do so. A man who's just as exhausted and unmotivated to meet new people. A man who's also stopped making any kind of advances towards women, who doesn't want to have to make too much effort. Everything's got to come to him, and if it doesn't then it's not going to happen. Tell her, 'That's Leo for you, Mia!' But don't say, 'You're going to love him,' because that presupposes that we might actually have to look each other in the eye. And at the moment I suspect that would be too much 'relationship effort' for both of us.

(I'm also slightly put out by how swiftly you're handing me over to your best friend. Emmi, where's your jealousy?)

Forty minutes later

Re:

Oh Leo, spare me the jealousy talk! I can't 'own' you beyond your messages in my inbox. Anyway, if you were to 'belong' to one of my best friends, then you'd belong to me a bit too. (Do you really think I'd set you up without considering what I might get out of it myself?) I've told Mia about you plenty of times. Do you want to know what she thinks? (I wouldn't put it past you to say: No, I'm not interested. But I'm going to tell you anyway.) She said, 'You see, Emmi, that's the kind of man I'd like, someone who'd rather get an e-mail from me than have sex. All men want sex. But it's a classy man who'd actually prefer the former!'

Five minutes later
Re:
You're back on sex again, Emmi!

Three minutes later
Re:
Thanks, I noticed that too. It's because I've immersed myself in the male domain.

Eight minutes later
Re:
It seems that you're keen to immerse yourself, so you can write uninhibitedly about sex.

166

Six minutes later

Re:

Don't be so sanctimonious, Leo! Have you forgotten your drunken e-mail about the blindfolds and your hungover leching the next day? You're not exactly the sexless preacher type, even though sometimes that's how you'd like to come across! So should I arrange a meeting between you and Mia or not?

Three minutes later

Re:

You're not serious are you?

One minute later

Re:

Of course I'm serious! I'm convinced that neither you nor Mia would need to 'make too much effort' to hit it off straightaway. Trust me — I know what makes people tick.

Seven minutes later

Re:

Thank you, but no thanks. It would be a little

perverse if I met Emmi's friend rather than Emmi.

Goodnight!

YOUR Leo (still)

Eight minutes later

Re:

But you don't want to meet me in person!

Goodnight to you (also still and for ever more)

YOUR Emmi (sort of)

Fifty seconds later

Subject: (no subject)

Oh, and there's one other thing: I haven't even got started on your remarks about 'happily married' in inverted commas! Take that as a warning.

Sleep well, my friend.

Emmi

The following evening

Subject: ???

Won't I get any e-mails from Leo today? Is he

angry with me? About Mia?

Night night,

Emmi

The following morning

Subject: Mia

Good morning, Emmi.

I've had a good think about your offer. If you arrange it, and if your friend Mia really wants to, then I will meet her!

Best wishes,

Leo

Fifteen minutes later

Re:

Leeeeoooo? Are you winding me up?

Half an hour later

Re:

No, not at all. I mean it. I'll happily meet Mia for a coffee. Be so kind as to sort out all the logistics, dear Emmi. Saturday or Sunday afternoon would suit. A café somewhere in the centre would be good. Either

Café Huber again, or Europa, or Café Paris, I don't mind.

Forty minutes later

Re:

You're so weird, Leo. Why the sudden change of heart? Are you sure you're not making fun of me? Do you really want me to ask Mia? Promise me you won't pull out at the last minute. Mia's not the kind of woman you can play games with.

Three hours later

Re:

And I'm not the kind of man who plays games with a woman he doesn't know; at least not those sorts of games. I just changed my mind, that's all. Why should I not meet a woman who comes with such a warm recommendation? I can't object to a non-committal hour of chat. The more I think about it, Emmi, the more I like your arrangement.

Have a nice evening,

Leo

Ten minutes later

Re:

Now I'm starting to think about my role in all this, Leo! I'll call Mia and let you know.

A minute and a half later

Re:

What role are you thinking about, and why?

Twenty minutes later

Re:

Dear Leo,

I suspect you're convinced that I'm the one who's going to pull out. Because you think I've never had any intention of introducing you to my friend — and an extremely attractive friend at that. You think 'Mia' is all a ruse to make myself seem more interesting to you, am I right? Well you're wrong, my dear Leo! I'm going to call Mia now, and if she says yes, you'd better make sure you do meet. Otherwise I'll be seriously pissed off!

But for now, much love,

Emmi

But Mia will say no. Because Mia won't understand why she should go on a date with a stranger who's a friend of her friend — what's more, a friend who her friend has never even met. Mia will ask herself, quite rightly, why she should meet this man. Mia will feel like a guinea pig. But I'm happy to be proved wrong. Goodnight, send my regards to the wine cabinet! When 'Operation Mia' has been concluded we can raise another glass of wine to us, Emmi. How about that?

The next day

Subject: Date with Mia

Hello Leo,

How are you? *So* hot today. I don't know what else I can take off. Do you ever wear shorts and sandals? Do you prefer T-shirts or polo shirts, or a perfectly ironed shirt? How many buttons do you leave undone? Jeans, chinos or — gulp! — Bermudas? How bright does it have to be before you'll wear sunglasses? Do you have hairy forearms? What about a hairy chest? — O.K., O.K., I'll stop there.

172

What I wanted to say was that I called Mia. In principle she'd be happy to meet you for a coffee one day. 'Why not?' she said. But you'll have to phone her. (Which you won't, of course.) Mia doesn't believe that you want to meet her at all — she thinks it's a ruse by her friend Emmi who's desperate to get her together with someone. And she wants to know what you look like. He's not ugly, I told her, at least I don't think he is. But I've only seen his sister ... Well, this is all a bit laborious. I'm sure nothing will come of it. I hope you survive today's heatwave!

Your Emmi

Two and a half hours later

Re:

Dear Emmi,

In response to your questions, I'm absolutely fine. Terribly hot, actually! When you write, 'I don't know what else I can take off,' you want me to imagine what Emmi looks like when she has no idea what to take off. You've won, Emmi, I'm imagining it now!

I only wear shorts on the beach. (But there isn't one here, is there?) Sandals: never, but if you want I could put some on — for our first meeting. T-shirt or shirt? Both, often one over the other. Buttons undone? Depends on the weather. Right now all my buttons are open, but then again no-one's watching. Trousers? Jeans rather than chinos. Bermudas? Definitely for our first meeting, Emmi, as long as it happens in summer (sometime in the next few years)! Sunglasses? When it's sunny. Hair? Head, chin, sideburns, arms, legs, chest . . . are you getting the picture?

Oh, yes, Mia. Could I have her number, please?

Enjoy the heat.

Yours,

Leo

Forty-five seconds later

Re:

What? Are you seriously going to phone her? You still think I'm bluffing, don't you? Here you are then: 0773 863 6271. Mia Lechberger. Happy now?

An hour and a half later

Re:

Thanks, Emmi. Extraordinary to be sweating

so much at the end of May . . . I'm off to a two-day conference in Budapest. I'll write as soon as I'm back. Take care, Emmi.

Love,

Leo

Two days later

Subject: (no subject)

Hi Leo,

Are you back? Guess who I spoke to this morning? And guess what she told me? 'Your e-mail friend phoned me. I was so surprised I nearly hung up. But he was really nice! Such a polite, friendly guy, a bit shy, charming . . . blah blah blah, yadda yadda . . . And he's got such a lovely voice! And such a nice accent . . . ' Leo, Leo, you must have pulled out all the stops. I have to admit, I never thought you'd actually call her. I hope you have fun when you meet up tomorrow!

By the way, Mia asked if I'd like to come too. I replied that you definitely wouldn't be happy with that. I told her that I'm a kind of fantasy figure to you, a woman with three faces, none of which he's set eyes on. He doesn't want to have to commit to any one of them. It's true, isn't it?

Much love,
Emmi

Three days later
Re:

Hello Emmi,

I'm back, but I'm sorry to say I'm still frantically busy. Your friend Mia sounds really nice on the phone. I'll be in touch,

Leo

P.S. You don't have to make a personal appearance, Emmi. I assume Mia will relay all the details of our meeting while they're still fresh.

Twelve minutes later
Re:

You've been so mischievous recently, Leo. I really don't know what to think. Well, good luck!

Emmi

P.S. See ya! (In my next life.)

6

Three days later
Subject: (no subject)
Hi Leo,
How's it going?
Love,
Emmi

Fifteen minutes later
Re:
Hi Emmi,
Yes, not bad. How about you?

Eight minutes later
Re:
Good, thanks. Apart from the heat. Is this normal for the end of May? 35 degrees in May — has it ever been that hot in the past? I'm sure it hasn't! And otherwise? Everything O.K.?

Twenty minutes later

Re:

Yes, thanks Emmi, everything's fine just now. You're right — the temperature used to get up to 35 degrees at the end of July, beginning of August, perhaps one or two days a year, no more than that. O.K., maybe it was for four or five days. But not in May, it's never been like this in May! I tell you, global warming is going to become a hot topic. It's not just some campaign launched by bored climate researchers. I reckon we're going to have to get used to hot summers every year.

Three minutes later

Re:

You're right, Leo, the variations in temperature are getting more and more extreme. And how are you spending these steamy days and nights?

Fourteen minutes later

Re:

And we're going to have more frequent and violent storms. Mudslides, floods. There'll be periods of drought too. Do you know what that means? It would be foolish to underestimate the economic and ecological consequences of climate change.

Five minutes later

Re:

Pineapples growing in the Alps. Compulsory snow chains for all cars in Apulia. Paddy fields on the Faroes. Stalls selling anti-freeze in Damascus. Colonies of camels in Murmansk. Yacht clubs in the Sahara.

Eighteen minutes later

Re:

Soon you'll be able to fry eggs without a cooker in the Scottish Highlands, assuming free-range chickens don't come pre-roasted and lay hard-boiled eggs, even in winter.

Two minutes later

Re:

Stop Leo, I can't take any more. I give up: How did it go? And please please please don't now ask me: 'How did what go?' Let's try to save ourselves a few keystrokes, O.K.?

Thirteen minutes later

Re:

You mean my Sunday meeting with Mia? It was nice! Very nice, in fact. Thanks for asking.

One minute later

Re:

What do you mean 'Sunday meeting'? Does that mean there's been a 'Monday meeting' too?

Eight minutes later

Re:

Yes, Emmi, funnily enough we met up again yesterday evening. We went out for an Italian. Do you know La Spezia in Kenienstrasse? It's got a fabulously intimate courtyard. Perfect in this heat. Best of all, it's very quiet with good, unobtrusive music and excellent wines from Piedmont. I can heartily recommend La Spezia.

Fifty seconds later

Re:

Did you click?

Eighteen minutes later

Re:

Did we click? You always use these technical terms! You'd better ask Mia. She's one of your best friends, after all. She even says she *is* your best friend. I'm afraid I've got to sign off for today, Emmi. Let's e-mail again tomorrow. Goodnight. I hope your bedroom's not oppressively hot.

Three minutes later

Re:

But it's not late, Leo. Have you got something on this evening? Are you meeting up with Mia? If you do see her today, could you ask her to give me a call? I can't seem to get hold of her. Have a nice, hot evening, and enjoy yourself.

Emmi

P.S. And here's a tip: definitely bring up climate change. I'm sure Mia could listen to you talk about it for hours, you make it sound so fascinating.

Two minutes later

Re:

I'm not seeing Mia again until tomorrow. I'm just whacked today and I want to go to bed early. Goodnight, I'm shutting down now.

Leo

Thirty seconds later

Re:

Night.

Three days later

Subject: (no subject)

Hi Emmi,

Are you looking out of the window too? Spooky, isn't it? A hailstorm's like a taste of the end of the world. You've got this strange, ochre veil hanging over the sky, all of a sudden it's covered by a dark-grey curtain, and then billions of these white pebbles hurtle to earth at breakneck speed. What's that film called where it rains toads, or frogs, or chickens? Do you, by any chance, know?

Love,

Leo

Re:

Animal Farm. The Frog Prince. Kentucky Fried Chicken — I don't hear from you for three days, and then I get these effusive mini-lectures on meteorology. It's driving me nuts! Please e-mail them to someone else. Do you think I've stuck with you in my inbox these past six months, and do you imagine that I've spent God knows how many hours a day for the past weeks and months, just so we can now start discussing heavy showers and ochre veils hanging over the sky? If you've got something to tell me about yourself, go ahead. If there's anything you want to know about me, ask away. But I've got better things to do than correspond about the weather. Has Mia turned your head so far that all you can now see is hailstones? I've got a couple more questions, since we're on the subject. Did you ask her to keep quiet about your dates for the moment?

What's that all about, some kind of silly adolescent secretiveness? An information blackout? What a childish little game. If I'm going to be honest, Leo, that's really spoiled all the pleasure of e-mailing with you.

Have a nice day,

Emmi

Two hours later

Re:

Dear Emmi,

I've known Mia for less than a week. We've met four times. We hit it off straight away. We get on like a house on fire, mostly. But it's far too early to predict how things will progress. And it's far too early to 'go live' with it, do you know what I'm saying? Mia and I have to be clear about our feelings for each other first. To what extent are they influenced by the circumstances in which we met? Are they just temporary, or might they have a future? These are questions which we have to answer for ourselves. So please be patient, Emmi. I'll tell you everything in due course. And I imagine that Mia feels the same, precisely because you're her best friend. Just give us a little time. I hope you understand.

Best regards,

Leo

Ten minutes later

Re:

Dear Leo,

You can't see me or hear me right now, so let me tell you that as I write this I'm feeling

184

cool, calm and collected. I'm not in the least irritated, hysterical or aggressive. Oh no. The following words are written with utter composure and serenity:

Leo, that's the shittiest e-mail I've ever read. Goodbye!

Fifteen minutes later

Re:

Well then I'm terribly sorry for you, Emmi. I'd better stop writing to you for the time being. When you're in the mood to get back in contact with the mouthpiece of your 'other world', just write to me.

Love,

Leo

Five days later

Subject: Yearning . . .

Hi Leo,

How are all your 'things' developing? Have you and Mia managed to sort out your feelings for each other yet? Do you now know what's just 'temporary' and what might 'have a future'? Have you now answered a few questions 'for yourselves'?

I miss the old Leo who said what there was to say and felt what there was to feel. I really yearn for him!!!

Have a nice day,

Emmi

P.S. You probably know about Mia and me. Now that I'm aware she doesn't know what to say to me either, I've asked her to consider Leo Leike a taboo subject.

Three hours later

Re:

Dear Emmi,

That last comment was a subtle piece of understatement. If I'm correctly informed, what you actually said to your friend Mia on the phone the other day was, 'Either you tell me everything about you and Leo, or nothing at all. If you choose the latter, I suggest we give our long-standing friendship a break for a few months.'

What's wrong with you, Emmi? I don't get it. After all, it was *you* who brought Mia and me together. *You* were the one who insisted I met her. *You* thought we'd make a dream couple. Why are you now being so cynical and malicious? Were you too sure of me, Leo, as a supplement to your emotional life, as your possession outside your family? Are you now angry because you think you've lost your virtual property to your best friend?

Emmi, for months you were the person I was closest to. And I was (I still am) happy that our attempts at a 'physical' meeting have consistently failed. I don't care what you look like, as long as I can see you as I want to see you. I'm grateful I don't have to find out that in reality you're a different person from 'Emmi the heroine in my e-mail novel'. Like this you're perfect, no-one can touch you.

But Emmi, this is why our relationship can't progress any further. Everything else is happening beyond our computer screens. The best proof of this is Mia. I'll be honest with you, in the beginning I was quite hurt that you wanted to get me together with her. My first meeting was more of an act of defiance against you, Emmi. But I soon understood the difference between you and her. You, Emmi, don't even dare describe your piano because it's got no place at all in my world. By contrast, half a metre away from me Mia leans forward over a tiny table and winds *spaghetti al pesto* around her fork. When she turns her head to one side I can feel the gust of air this produces. I can see, hear, touch and smell her all at the same time. Mia is a physical being. Emmi is fantasy. They each have their advantages and disadvantages.

Have a nice evening,

Leo

Half an hour later

Re:

My piano is black, rectangular, and is made almost entirely of wood. Part of it juts out horizontally and if you lift the curved, black lid you'll find some black and white keys. I should really know how many of each there are, but I'm ashamed to admit I'd have to count them. Can I give you an exact figure later, Leo? I do know that the white keys are a bit bigger, and there are more of them. If I press a key, a sound comes out somewhere near the top of the piano. You never know *exactly* where it comes from though. You can't really check when you're playing. Much more important is the sound it makes. If I choose a key to the left, it produces a deep tone. And the further a key is to the right, the higher the sound when I press it. If I press several black keys many times in succession, I get a simple, Chinese tune, a bit like a children's song from the Far East. If you'd like me to tell you any more about the white keys and what you can do with them, just ask. But I think I've managed to explain the most important features of my piano. There you go, I've dared to describe my piano to you!

Devotedly yours,

Emmi

Five minutes later

Re:

Nicely done, Emmi. I think I've got a good idea of your piano now. I can even picture it right here in front of me, in fact. And you, Emmi, are sitting at it, counting the keys. Thanks for letting me watch! Goodnight.

One hour later

Subject: (no subject)

Hi Leo, it's me again. I'm not tired yet. And basically I don't know what to say. I just feel sad. I thought Mia might bring us closer to one another, physically as well. But instead it seems she's forcing us further apart. And I can't even blame her for it, because it was my idea. I'm going to be honest with you: I did want you to meet each other, I admit, but I didn't want you two to get together. To me you two were (you still are!) anything but a 'dream couple'. I was too sure of what I thought about you, Leo. I thought I knew you. I didn't think it possible that you would fall in love with her. There's no doubt that Mia is attractive. But she's about as different from me as anyone could be. She's a sportswoman through and through, she's strong, she's lithe, she's sinewy. Even her moles have had the full workout, and her armpit hair is probably pure muscle. You can hardly see her breasts for her ribcage. And her sun-wrinkled skin is one big coconut-oil refinery. Mia is fitness personified. For her, sex must be like a combination of press-ups and pelvic-floor exercises, interspersed with breathers to allow for her orgasms. She might be one for a surfboard, for therapeutic fasting, for the New York marathon. But she'd never be the woman for Leo — at least that's what I thought. I imagined you very differently, Leo. If you lust after Mia, you reject me. Can you understand why I might find that depressing?

Ten minutes later
Re:

Who says I'm lusting after Mia? Who says she's lusting after me?

190

Two minutes later

Re:

You do, Leo! You! You say it! And the way you say it, it's hideous! You couldn't say it more hideously than you did in your icky, noxious, we-have-to-be-clear-about-our-feelings-for-each-other e-mail. 'In many ways we're incredibly alike,' you say. Yuck! — I'd never have thought you capable of *that*, Leo!

Five minutes later

Re:

But it's true — Mia and I *are* incredibly alike in many ways. I'm not making any of this up. For example, our observations and opinions about you, dear Emmi Rothner, are strikingly similar!

Three minutes later

Re:

Please don't tell me you slept with her.

Four minutes later

Re:

Emmi, you're behaving like a man again, aren't you? Stick to the subject. It's

191

completely irrelevant whether or not I've slept with Mia.

Fifty-five seconds later
Re:

Irrelevant?? Not to me it isn't! Anyone who sleeps with Mia is never going to sleep with me, not even on a spiritual level. And I mean that.

Two minutes later
Re:

Don't always reduce our relationship to the mere fact that on the odd occasion we've slept with each other spiritually.

Fifty seconds later
Re:

So you've slept with me spiritually? First I've heard of it. Sounds good though!

One minute later
Re:

Talking of sleep, now it's time for the real thing. Goodnight, Emmi — it's two o'clock in the morning.

Thirty seconds later

Re:

I know, isn't it great? Just like old times!

Night night,

Emmi

The next morning

Subject: Not a word about sex

Good morning, Leo. What observations and opinions about me did you trade with Mia? What did Mia tell you? Do you now know which of the three Emmis with size 37 shoes I am? Am I at least the Emmi your sister said you could fall in love with?

An hour and a half later

Re:

You're not going to believe this, Emmi, but we were talking about your personality, not your appearance. Right from the start I explained to Mia that I didn't want to know what you looked like. Her reply was, 'Well, you're missing something!' (She really *is* a good friend.) Of course, Mia knew too that the last thing you wanted was for her and me to get together. It took no time at all for us to understand the roles we'd been allocated. After only ten minutes in each other's company we were allies in all matters pertaining to Emmi Rothner.

Twelve minutes later

Re:

And then you deliberately fell in love with each other.

One minute later

Re:

Who says?

Eight minutes later

Re:

Leo Leike says: 'Half a metre away from me Mia leans forward over a tiny table and winds *spaghetti al pesto* around her fork.' Sighs. 'When she turns her head to one side I can feel the gust of air this produces.' Sighs. 'I can see, hear, touch and smell her all at the same time.' Sighs. 'Mia is a physical being.' Swoons. Do you know what, Leo? With Marlene I forgive you. She came before me, she has prior rights. But Mia's gusts when she

194

turns her head — what a cheek! I'd like to be able to turn my head too and produce a gust of air for you to feel, Maestro Leo! (O.K., I take the 'Maestro' bit back.) What do Mia's gusts have that mine don't? I can generate fabulous gusts of air when I turn my head, and you'd better believe it.

Twenty minutes later
Re:

We also talked about your marriage, Emmi.

Three minutes later
Re:

Oh really? Getting back on to our favourite subject, are we? And what does Mia have to say about it? Did she admit to you that she can't stand Bernhard?

Fifteen minutes later
Re:

No, not at all. She had only positive things to say about him. She says that your marriage is *the* model marriage. It's spooky, she says, but everything about it is just perfect. She says that ever since Emmi's been with Bernhard, her vulnerabilities have just disappeared. She's forgotten how to show any weakness. When she turns up somewhere with Bernhard and the two children, it's as if the dream family has arrived. They're all smiling, all friendly, all happy. You and your husband don't even need to talk to each other — a peaceful harmony reigns. Even the kids just sit and hug each other. The perfect idyll. When friends invite the Rothners round, they'd best book themselves in for a few hours of therapy afterwards, Mia says. Other people immediately think they've done everything wrong. They feel like failures. Either because their partners are no longer supportive, or they don't like the look of them any more — or both. Or they've got children who terrorize them. Or all three. Or they've got none of the above — they've got nobody. Like Mia, Mia says. And it makes her miserable, but only if she compares herself to Emmi.

Eighteen minutes later

Re:

Well, I know what Mia thinks about my marriage and my family life. She doesn't like Bernhard because she feels he's taken something away from her: me, her best friend. It's true, damn it, she really suffers from the fact that things are no longer going as badly for me as they are for her. Not badly enough for me to go and have a cry on her shoulder. Our friendship has become very one-sided: we had more in common before. We shared the same troubles, the same adversaries — men and their flaws, for example. That was extremely fertile ground, we could go on for hours about it, we had an embarrassment of riches there. But when I met Bernhard everything changed. For the life of me I can't find anything bad to say about him. There's no point in me pretending I'm annoyed about stupid little things just so that I can affect some kind of solidarity with Mia. So we find ourselves in fundamentally different lives. That's our problem.

Five minutes later

Re:

Mia says there's just one thing she's aware of which doesn't conform to the image of the Rothner family idyll. At least she can't make any sense of it, even though she's talked to you about it a lot.

Fifty seconds later

Re:

And what would that be?

Forty seconds later

Re:

Me.

Thirty seconds later

Re:

You?

Fifteen minutes later

Re:

Yes, me, us, Emmi. Mia can't understand why you write to me, the way you write to me, what you write to me, and how often you write to me, etc. She can't understand why you find contact with me so important. She says, 'There's nothing missing from Emmi's life, absolutely nothing. If she's got problems she knows she can come to me or talk to one of her other girlfriends. If she's looking for an ego boost, all she has to do is to stroll through the pedestrian zone. If she wants to flirt, she could give out numbered tickets in the street and call up the men one after the other. She doesn't need some time-consuming, energy-zapping, ever-intense e-mail correspondent.' The point is, Emmi, Mia doesn't know why you need me, or what possible good I can be to you.

Two minutes later
Re:
And don't you know either, Leo?

Nine minutes later
Re:
Yes, I think I do. I take you at your word. I've tried to explain to Mia that I'm a sort of 'outpost' for Emmi, a minor distraction from her family life. I'm somebody who appreciates and likes her for who she is, without her having to be around. All she has to do is write, nothing more. She says, 'Emmi doesn't need a distraction. She'd never put herself out for a 'distraction'. If Emmi makes an effort it's because she 'wants' something. And when Emmi wants something, she doesn't just want a lot of it. If Emmi wants something, she wants it *all*.'

Three minutes later

Re:

Maybe Mia doesn't know me so well after all. What do you think she means by 'it all'. We haven't eaten *spaghetti al pesto* together. I haven't even turned my head to generate a gust of air that you could feel, my dear Leo. Evidently my friend Mia is ahead of me by some stretch on that front. I'd really rather not know how much closer she is to having 'it all' than I am.

One minute later

Re:

I'm delighted that you don't want to know, just for a change.

Fifty seconds later

Re:

So how close did she get to having 'it all', then?

Two minutes later

Re:

It depends on what you mean by 'it all'.

Fifty-five seconds later

Re:

You see, Leo, that's the kind of splendid answer that justifies the effort of my e-mails. You're welcome to pass that on to my friend Mia. When are you seeing her next? Today?

Three minutes later

Re:

No, this evening I've been invited to dinner by some colleagues. I should be getting ready soon. Have a nice evening, Emmi.

Forty-five seconds later

Re:

Aren't you taking Mia with you? She's obviously not that close to having 'it all' with you, then.

One minute later

Re:

No, not so close, Emmi, if that makes you feel any better.

Forty seconds later
Re:
It certainly does!

Fifty seconds later
Re:
Emmi. Emmi. Emmi.

The following day
Subject: Mia
Hi Leo,
I'm seeing Mia tomorrow!
All the best,
Emmi

Ten minutes later
Re:
Hi Emmi.
That's nice for you, and nice for Mia, too.
All the best to you,
Leo

Fifty seconds later
Re:

Is that all you've got to say?

Twenty minutes later
Re:

What did you imagine, Emmi? Should I have panicked? It's not parents' evening, Emmi. I haven't been skiving off school. Mia's not my teacher, and you're not my mother. So I've got nothing to be worried about.

Three minutes later
Re:

Leo, if you and Mia are, you know . . . then I'd rather hear it from you today than find out from Mia tomorrow. So will you please tell me?

Four minutes later
Re:

Am I sleeping with Mia? If I am, Mia might not want you to know.

A minute and a half later

Re:

You're the one who doesn't want me to know. Well tough, Leo, I know already! Judging by the way you write, you must be sleeping with her.

Thirteen minutes later

Re:

Would that be so awful for you? Would that turn your entire 'other world' upside down? Or is it just that old childhood thing: if I can't have it, my best friend won't have it either?

Four minutes later

Re:

I think you're being a bit immature about all this, Leo. Let's just leave it.

Have a pleasant day.

Read you soon,

Emmi

Ten minutes later
Re:

And you used to be jollier, my dear. Yes, read you soon, no doubt.

The following day
Subject: Mia

Hi Leo, I met up with Mia!

Half an hour later
Re:

I know, Emmi. You said you were going to.

Two minutes later
Re:

Don't you want to know how it went?

Four minutes later
Re:

Good question. There are two possible answers. Either 1) Mia will tell me. Or 2) You, Emmi, are going to tell me about it now anyway. I choose 2).

One minute later
Re:

Close, but the wrong answer. Ask Mia how it went. Have a nice afternoon!

Seven hours later
Re:

Goodnight, Emmi. That was a pretty poor performance today.

The next day
Subject: Emmi?

My dear e-mail partner, have I offended you? Would you mind telling me how? Did Mia tell you something you didn't want to hear?

Two and a half hours later
Re:

You know exactly what Mia told me, Leo, and you know exactly what she *didn't* tell me. 'Yes, he's sweet,' she said. 'Yes, we get on well. Yes, we see each other quite a bit. Yes, sometimes it gets pretty late (smirk, giggle). Yes, he's alright (stupid grin). Yes, he's the kind of man (sigh) you could imagine (swoon) ... But Emmi, so what if we're sleeping together? ... Oh Emmi, why do you always have to talk about sex?' etc etc.

My dear Leo, that's not what she's like. The Mia I know can talk about sex for hours on end! She describes every muscle that's exerted or involved in any way, even if it's just for watching (or listening). As a sports scientist, Mia can divide up one single, five-second orgasm into seven separate working stages, complete with tables of calories burned etc, each one requiring an hour-long presentation. That's Mia! And do you know what completely *isn't* Mia? — 'Oh Emmi, why do you always have to talk about sex!' That's not Mia at all, not a bit. That's 100 per cent Leo Leike. What have you done to Mia? And why? Just to annoy me?

Thirteen minutes later
Re:

Didn't Mia ask you why you're so interested in whether I'm having sex with her? Didn't she tell you that she never asks how often you sleep with your Bernhard? (O.K., I take back the 'your'.) Did Mia not ask you what you actually want from me? Well, didn't she? And what did you tell her?

Fifty seconds later
Re:

That I want e-mails from him! (But not ones like that.)

A minute and a half later
Re:

You can't always pick and choose.

Three minutes later
Re:

I don't want to have to pick and choose. I want them all to be lovely. You used to write me such lovely e-mails, Leo. But since you've been sleeping with Mia, all you do is beat about the bush. Fine, it's all my fault, I shouldn't have introduced you to her. My mistake.

Eight minutes later
Re:

Dear Emmi,

I promise you'll get another nice e-mail from me, Mia or no Mia. But I can't manage one today. I'm going to the theatre (no, not with

Mia, but with my sister and a few friends).

Have a nice evening. And say hi to your piano.

Leo

Five hours later

Subject: (no subject)

Are you back? I can't sleep. By the way, have I ever told you about the north wind? I can't stand it when the north wind blows through my window. It'd be nice if you'd drop me a line. You could say, 'Why don't you just close your window then?' And then I could tell you: 'Because I can't sleep with the window closed.'

Five minutes later

Re:

Do you sleep with your head by the window?

Fifty seconds later

Re:

LEO!!!! Yes, I sleep with my head right by the window.

Forty-five seconds later

Re:

What about turning 180 degrees and sleeping with your toes by the window?

Fifty seconds later

Re:

That wouldn't work. I wouldn't have my bedside table and reading light.

One minute later

Re:

But you don't need a light to sleep.

Thirty seconds later

Re:

No, but I do to read.

One minute later

Re:

So read, and then turn round and sleep with your toes by the window.

Forty seconds later

Re:

If I turned round I'd be wide awake again, and then I'd have to read a bit more to get to sleep. But I wouldn't have my little bedside table with the reading light.

Thirty seconds later

Re:

Simple! Just put it at the other end of the bed.

Thirty-five seconds later

Re:

Wouldn't work, the flex is too short.

Forty seconds later

Re:

Shame. I've got an extension lead here.

Twenty-five seconds later

Re:

Send it over!

211

Forty-five seconds later

Re:

O.K., I'll send it as a word file.

Fifty seconds later

Re:

Got it, thanks. What a great extension, really long! I'll just plug it in.

Forty seconds later

Re:

Be careful you don't trip over it in the night.

Thirty-five seconds later

Re:

Ah, now I'm going to sleep really soundly, thanks to you and your extension.

One minute later

Re:

Now the north wind can blow as hard as it likes.

Forty-five seconds later

Re:

I really, really like you, Leo. You're a brilliant solution to the north wind!

Thirty seconds later

Re:

I like you a lot, too, Emmi. Goodnight.

Twenty-five seconds later

Re:

Night night. Sweet dreams.

The following evening

Subject: (no subject)

Good evening, Emmi. Were you waiting for me to write first?

Five minutes later

Re:

I usually wait for you to write first, Leo, but mostly in vain. This time I held out. How are you doing?

Three minutes later

Re:

I'm fine. I've spoken to Mia. And we've decided to tell you everything about us, if you still want to know.

Eight minutes later

Re:

Only when I know will I know whether I want to know. But given that you're being so formal about it, it's highly probable that when I know, I'll know I didn't really want to know after all. If it's some love story involving a pregnancy, a trip to Venice and a wedding date, you'd best spare me. I've already had a row with a client today. And I've got my period.

Four minutes later

Re:

No, it's not a love story. It never was. I'm amazed you ever thought it might be. To start off with you were pretty confident about your arrangement. 'Your arrangement' — that's the point. Would you like me to go into details?

Six minutes later

Re:

That's not fair, Leo! I wasn't confident about any arrangement. There *was* no 'arrangement'. I didn't even consider what might happen if you got in touch with my friend. I was just curious to know what she would talk about — and what you would say, Leo. It was only when you told me, or rather *didn't* tell me, that I realized how little I liked what you talked about, or rather *didn't* talk about, you and Mia. But go ahead, tell me more. You've already written the most important sentence anyway. (The first one.) Not much can happen now.

An hour and a half later

Re:

Mia and I met for the first time that Sunday afternoon in the café. We knew at once why we were sitting there — not because of us, but because of you. There was no chance of us getting closer, let alone falling in love with each other. We were anything but 'meant for each other', the very opposite in fact. We felt like your puppets from the outset, like pawns that you, dear Emmi, had just put in play. But we didn't understand the 'game'. And we still

215

can't understand it now. Emmi. You know that Mia thinks the world of you, admires you, even envies you; is that supposed to make me more interested in you? If so, then why? Do I need to know how perfect and idyllic your family life is? Why? What has that got to do with our e-mails? Does it stop the north wind from blowing through your window? Does it stop you from getting to sleep?

And Mia. She feels she doesn't know where she stands with you any more. One thing was clear to her from the beginning: I was taboo for her. I had a sign round my neck saying, 'This belongs to Emmi! Do not touch!' Mia felt that all she could do was listen to me. She was expected to give you a detailed description of me, she was supposed to bring you the other side of me, the physical side you don't know, to give you a rounded picture.

Well, Emmi, Mia and I weren't prepared to play the roles you'd allocated to us. We were determined to put a spanner in the works of your weird game. We were defiant — and even though we didn't fall in love, we did sleep together. It did us the world of good, we had fun, we were both up for it. There was no fluttering of the heart, there wasn't much desire, and no great passion either. We decided to do it because of you — that was reason enough. It was the simplest and truest thing in the world, because we were seriously pissed off with you! So we played our own game within the game. It worked for one night, but not for a second. In the long run you can only sleep 'with each other', not against a third party. And it was obvious that Mia and I would never come to anything. But we were happy to meet up, it was nice to chat, in fact we liked each other (and still do), and we enjoyed keeping you at a distance, Emmi. As a little punishment for your arrogance.

So that's the story. I'm dying to know whether you'll understand this, and how you're going to digest it, dearest email partner. And now it's night. A full moon, as far as I can tell. And the north wind has eased off. You can sleep with your head by the window.

Goodnight!

Two days later
Subject: (no subject)
Dear Emmi,

It's miserable to be left hanging for two days as I've been left hanging. That's what's you've done, you've left me in mid-air. So may I politely invite you to reply. By all means bring me down to earth, but don't leave me in mid-air.

Yours sincerely,

Leo

The following day

Subject: Digestion

Hi Leo,

Jonas dislocated his arm playing volleyball. We've just spent two nights in hospital. That's just a little taste of our family idyll.

Now, digestion: I tried to digest your e-mail on several occasions, but unfortunately it keeps coming back up. Now it's just a tasteless mush. You ask whether I wanted you to find out from Mia how perfect and idyllic my family life is. My dear Leo, you and Mia are labouring under a vast misapprehension. My family life is good, but by no means perfect. 'Family life' as such has very little to do with perfection, and a great deal to do with endurance, patience, indulgence and children's dislocated arms. And here allow me to draw on my years of experience, which — I'm sorry to say — you and Mia lack.

'Family idyll' is an oxymoron: you can have family, or idyll, but not both.

And I've got something else to say about your 'game within a game'. So you and Mia slept together because you were pissed off with me, did you? It's been a long time since I heard anything so childish. Oh, Leo! Points deducted for that.

7

Two days later

Subject: Tidying up

Hi Emmi.

How are you? I'm not feeling that great. And I'm not particularly proud of myself either. I should never have met Mia. I should have known that, paradoxically, it would bind me closer to you, Emmi. I criticized you because I thought that was your intention. I take half of that back. I think we both intended it. It's just that neither of us has dared to admit it until now. Mia was our go-between. You put her on to me. And I got my revenge through her. It wasn't unfair on her. Mia's increasing interest in me is matched by an increasing interest in you, Emmi. I think it's up to you to get close to your friend again. And I ought to back off a bit. I need to do a little tidying up.

Have a good day,

Leo

One hour later

Re:

And what will you be tidying up next, Leo? Me?

Eight minutes later

Re:

I used to think that e-mails didn't need tidying up. But maybe, at some point, I ought to slowly put the brakes on.

Four minutes later

Re:

Here's Hesitant Leo in his element again: 'maybe', 'at some point', 'I ought', 'slowly put the brakes on'. Do you get a kick out of sharing your sheepish announcements about how you're going to step back from all this? Put the brakes on, Leo, for God's sake, but put them on properly!!! And stop tormenting me with your maybe, I ought, slowly . . . It's slowly beginning to annoy me!

Three minutes later
Re:
O.K., I'm putting the brakes on.

Forty seconds later
Re:
At last.

Thirty-five seconds later
Re:
Done.

Twenty-five seconds later
Re:
And now?

Two minutes later
Re:
Don't know. I'm waiting for it to stop.

Twenty-five seconds later
Re:
It has now. Night night!

Two days later

Subject: (no subject)

Hi Emmi,

So . . . are we not going to write to each other at all any more?

Seven hours later

Re:

Apparently not.

The following day

Subject: (no subject)

It's quite nice not getting any e-mails.

Two and a half hours later

Re:

Yes, I could get used to this.

Four hours later

Re:

Now we can see how exhausting it was.

Five and a half hours later
Re:
Stress. Sheer stress.

The following day
Subject: (no subject)
And how's Mia?

Two hours later
Re:
No idea, we're not seeing each other any more.

Eight hours later
Re:
Really? That's a shame.

Three minutes later
Re:
Yes, it is.

The following day

Subject: (no subject)

It's so much fun writing to you, Leo.

Nine hours later

Re:

Thanks, I can only return the compliment.

The following day

Subject: (no subject)

How's Marlene, by the way? Any relapses?

Three hours later

Re:

No, not yet, but I'm working on it. And what's your family up to? How's Jonas' knee?

Two hours later

Re:

Not knee, arm.

Five minutes later
Re:
Yes, of course, so sorry. How's his arm?

Three and a half hours later
Re:
Can't tell. It's in plaster.

Half an hour later
Re:
Oh, right, I see.

Two days later
Subject: (no subject)
It's sad, Emmi, we've got nothing more to say
to each other.

Ten minutes later
Re:
Maybe we never did.

Eight minutes later

Re:

Well, for two people who've got nothing to say to each other, we've been chatting away one hell of a lot.

Twenty minutes later

Re:

We haven't really said anything though. Nothing but empty words.

Five minutes later

Re:

If you say so.

Twelve minutes later

Re:

What a good thing that you put the brakes on.

Three minutes later

Re:

You're the one who said we'd stopped, Emmi!

Eight minutes later
Re:
And you say it every day.

Five hours later
Re:
Should we stop for good?

Three minutes later
Re:
I thought we already had.

Fifty seconds later
Re:
You really know how to get someone down.

Two minutes later
Re:
I learned that from you, Leo.
Goodnight.

Three minutes later
Re:
Goodnight.

Two minutes later
Re:
Goodnight.

One minute later
Re:
Goodnight.

Fifty seconds later
Re:
Goodnight.

Forty seconds later
Re:
Goodnight.

Twenty seconds later
Re:
Goodnight.

Two minutes later
Re:

It's three o'clock in the morning. Is the north wind blowing? Goodnight.

Fifteen minutes later
Re:

3.17. It's the west wind, leaves me cold. Goodnight.

The following morning
Subject: Good morning

Morning, Leo.

Three minutes later
Re:

Good morning, Emmi.

Twenty minutes later
Re:

This evening I'm off to Portugal for two weeks. A sun holiday with the children. Will you still be there when I get back, Leo? I need to know. When I say 'there' I mean . . . well, what do I mean? I mean, just there. Of course you understand what I mean. I'm afraid of losing you. Put on the brakes, by all means. Come to a stop, why not? I don't even mind empty words. But empty words *with* you, not without you!

Eighteen minutes later

Re:

Yes, my dear Emmi. I'm not going to wait around for you. But I will be here when you get back. I'm always here for you, even when we've come to a stop. Let's see how we feel after this two-week 'break'. It might do us good. I think the last few days have shown that we could do with one.

Love,

Leo

Two hours later

Re:

Just one thing before I leave. And please be honest, Leo! Have you lost interest in me?

Five minutes later

Re:

Do you really want me to be honest?

Eight minutes later

Re:

Yes, I really do. Be honest, and be quick! I have to take Jonas to get his plaster taken off.

Fifty seconds later

Re:

When an e-mail from you comes in, my heart begins to pound. I feel the same today as I did yesterday and seven months ago.

Forty seconds later

Re:

Despite all the empty words? That's so lovely!!! Holiday salvaged! Adieu.

Forty-five seconds later

Re:

Adieu.

Eight days later

Subject: (no subject)

Hi Leo,

I'm at an internet café in Porto. Just a quick note so that your heart doesn't stop pounding altogether from a lack of e-mails. We're all fine: the little one's had diarrhoea since the day we got here, the big one's fallen in love with a Portuguese surfing instructor. Only six days to go! Looking forward!

(P.S.: Don't start anything with Marlene!)

Six days later

Subject: Hi

Dear Leo,

I'm back. How was your 'break'? What's new? I missed you! You didn't write. Why not? I'm really nervous about getting your first e-mail. But I'm even more worried that you're going to keep me waiting for it. Question: where do we go from here?

Fifteen minutes later

Re:

Emmi,

You shouldn't be nervous of my first e-mail. Here it is — it's quite harmless.

1) What's new? — nothing.

2) The break was — long.

3) I didn't write because — we were having a break.

4) I missed you — too! (Probably more than you missed me. At least you had a sixteen-year-old daughter to protect from a Portuguese surfing instructor. How did the story end?)

5) Where do we go from here? There are three possibilities: carry on as before, stop, meet up.

Two minutes later

Re:

Re: 4) Fiona's going to emigrate to Portugal to marry the surfing instructor. She only came home to pack her stuff. Or so she thinks.

Re: 5) I'll go for — meeting up!

Three minutes later

Re:

Last night I had a vivid dream about you, Emmi.

Two minutes later

Re:

Really? That's happened to me too. I mean, I've had vivid dreams about you. But what exactly do you mean by 'vivid'? Was your dream just generally vivid, or was it erotic too?

Thirty-five seconds later

Re:

Yes, wildly erotic!

Forty-five seconds later

Re:

Are you serious? That doesn't sound like you at all.

One minute later

Re:

I know, I was surprised too.

Thirty seconds later

Re:

And??? I want details! What did we do? What did I look like? What was my face like?

One minute later

Re:

I didn't really register your face.

A minute and a half later

Re:

Oh Leo, what are you like! I bet I was the inscrutable blonde from the café, the one with the large breasts.

Fifty seconds later

Re:

What is it with you and large breasts? Do you have a problem with large breasts?

Two minutes later

Re:

You really amaze me, Leo. You're not interested in the size of my breasts, you just want to know whether or not I have a problem with large breasts. That's not what men are like! It almost makes me think you've got a full-blown large-breast problem.

Three minutes later

Re:

Call me asexual if you want, Emmi, but no matter whether they're large, small, thick, thin, broad, flat, round, oval, angular or square, I'm not interested in breasts when I don't know the face they come with. At any rate I lack the talent to be able to focus on the size of a woman's breasts in isolation.

One minute later

Re:

Ha! Now you're contradicting yourself! Three e-mails ago you told me about your extremely erotic dream, in which you were obviously able to see every little bit of me. Everything apart from my face, that is. Don't tell me you missed my breasts too.

237

Fifty-five seconds later
Re:

I didn't see a face or breasts, or any other part of your body. I just felt it all.

A minute and a half later
Re:

If you didn't see anything of me, how can you know that I was the woman you were blindly groping.

One minute later
Re:

Because there's only one woman who expresses herself like you do, and that's you!

Two and a half minutes later
Re:

So did we talk while you were groping me?

Fifty seconds later
Re:

I didn't grope you, I felt you — there's a vast difference. And (amongst other things) we talked.

Thirty-five seconds later
Re:
Extremely erotic!

A minute and a half later
Re:
What do you know about it, Emmi? I can see that you approach these things far too much like one of 'your' men.

Two minutes later
Re:
So on one side there are 'my men', and on the other, 'the one and only' Leo, the man who's too sublime for breasts. And for today let's end on this noble distinction. I have to stop now — there's some stuff I've got to sort out. I'll be in touch again tomorrow. Till then,

Emmi

The following day
Subject: Meeting up
Well, are we going to meet up? I've got all the time in the world. Bernhard's taken the

children on a week's walking holiday. I'm on my own.

Five and a half hours later
Re:
Hey, Leo, cat got your tongue?

Five minutes later
Re:
No, Emmi. I'm just thinking.

Ten minutes later
Re:
That does not bode well. I know exactly what you're thinking about. Please, Leo, let's meet up! Let's not miss what might be our last real opportunity to do so. What are you risking? What have *you* got to lose?

Two minutes later
Re:

1) You
2) Me
3) Us

Seventeen minutes later
Re:

The thought of actual contact seems to fill you with panic, Leo. We will see each other, and we'll like each other, and we'll talk to each other just as we always have, but this time with our mouths. We'll feel comfortable with each other from the word go, and after an hour we'll no longer be able to conceive of what it would have been like had we never set eyes on each other. We'll sit opposite each other at a small table in an Italian restaurant, and you can watch me eat *spaghetti al pesto*. (Do you mind if it's *vongole*?) I'll turn my head to one side and you'll be able to feel the gust of air that this produces, dear Leo. A real, physical, liberating, non-virtual gust of air!!!

An hour and a half later
Re:

You're not Mia, Emmi. Mia and I didn't have any expectations of each other. We set out as two people normally do when they meet. With us it's different, Emmi. We're starting off at the finishing line and there's only one way to go: backwards. We're heading for massive disillusionment. We can't live the things we write. We can't replace all those images we've painted of each other. It'll be a disappointment if you hide behind the Emmi I know. And that's what you'll do! You'll be depressed if I hide behind the Leo you know. And that's what I'll do! We'll come away from our first and only meeting feeling deflated, sluggish, as if we'd had a heavy meal that doesn't taste very good, a meal we'd been greedily looking forward to for a whole year, a dish we'd allowed to simmer and bubble away for months. And then what? Finished. All over. Polished off. Would we try to behave as if nothing had ever happened? In our minds we would always have the demythologized, uncovered, disenchanted, disappointed, raw reflection of the other person. We would no longer know what to write to each other. And at some point in the future we'd bump into each other in a café or on the underground. We would try to ignore each other, or pretend not to recognize each other; we would swiftly turn our backs on each other. We would be embarrassed by what had become of our 'us', what remained of it. Nothing. Two strangers with a shared pseudo-history, which shame-lessly they had allowed themselves to be deceived by for so long.

Three minutes later

Re:

And one hundred animal species become extinct every day.

One minute later

Re:

What's that supposed to mean?

Fifty-five seconds later

Re:

You just whinge, whinge, whinge, whinge, whinge. Paint things black, paint things black, paint things black, paint things black.

Twenty-five seconds later

Re:

Paint things black.

Forty seconds later

Re:

???

A minute and a half later
Re:

Paint things black. (You forgot one — five 'whinges', five 'paint things black'. Or four 'whinges', four 'paint things black' — you've got one too many 'whinges'.)

Two minutes later
Re:

Well spotted, nicely worked out. Typical Leo, a tiny bit O.C.D., but nonetheless decent and so sweetly attentive. But I want to see your eyes, your real eyes! Goodnight. Dream of me! And perhaps take a look at me while you're at it!

Three minutes later
Re:

Goodnight, Emmi. I'm sorry I am how I am, how I am, how I am.

Two days later
Subject: Meeting 'lite'

Good afternoon, Emmi. Are you (still) insulted, or do you fancy a few glasses of wine together tonight?

In hope, yours,

Leo

An hour and a half later

Re:

Hi Leo,

I'm meeting Mia in the flesh this evening. We've decided to hit town like we did in the good old days and keep on going until we lose it completely, or the last bar closes. Which means it might end up being five in the morning.

Sixteen minutes later

Re:

I understand. You need to make the most of it when the family's away. Give my regards to Mia. And have a good evening.

Eight minutes later

Re:

When you write e-mails like that one, and there aren't many of them, I'd rather *not* know what you look like. (And by the way you seem to have a pretty conventional idea of family life — or at least of *my* family life. *I* don't have to wait until my family's away to stay out until five in the morning. I can do that whenever I want.)

Three minutes later

Re:

And could you also meet up with me whenever you wanted? Irrespective of whether Bernhard was off in the mountains with the children for a week, or at home in the room next door (and could pop into your room any time)?

Twenty minutes later

Re:

FINALLY, THE TRUTH IS OUT!!! You could have spared us that gloomy sermon a couple of days ago about our devastating first meeting and our shattered images of each other. That's not your problem at all, is it? Your problem is Bernhard. You think you're far too important to be playing second fiddle to him. You don't want to meet me because in reality there's no way you can get together with me, whether you really want to or not.

On e-mail you can have me all to yourself — in the virtual world we get along just splendidly, and you can switch from intimate to distant just as you please. Am I right?

Forty-five minutes later

Re:

You haven't answered my question, Emmi. Would you (want to) meet me if your husband were sitting in the room next door? And (supplementary question) what would you tell him? Maybe, 'Hey hon, I'm meeting up with this guy tonight — we've been e-mailing each other for a year, usually several times a day from 'good morning' to 'goodnight'. He's often the first person to hear from me when I wake up. He's often the last person I speak to before I go to bed. And at night, when I can't sleep, when the north wind blows, I don't come to you, hon. No, I write this man an e-mail. And he writes back. You see, in my head this guy is damn good protection against the north wind. What do we write about? Oh, you know, personal stuff, just about us, about where the two of us would be if I didn't have you, hon, you and the kids. So, as I said, I'm meeting up with him tonight . . . '

Five minutes later
Re:

I never call my husband 'hon'.

Fifty seconds later
Re:

Oh, I'm sorry, Emmi. Of course, you say 'Bernhard'. That sounds much more respect-ful.

Four minutes later
Re:

Don't be angry with me for saying this, Leo, but you have a woeful perception of a smoothly functioning marriage. Do you know what I'd say to Bernhard if I met up with you one evening? I'd say: 'Bernhard, I'm going out tonight. I'm meeting a friend. I might be home late.' And do you know what Bernhard would say? 'Have fun, enjoy yourselves!' And do you know why he'd say that?

One minute later
Re:

Because he doesn't care what you do?

Forty seconds later
Re:
Because he trusts me!

One minute later
Re:
Trusts you in what way?

Fifty seconds later
Re:
He trusts me not to do anything which might jeopardize our relationship, now or in the future.

Nine minutes later
Re:
Oh yes, of course. You only expose yourself in your 'other world', which has minimal impact on your family. The real world remains untouched. Let's say you fell in love with me, Emmi, and I with you; let's say we had a romance, an affair, a passion . . . call it what you want. Does that still mean you're doing nothing that might jeopardize your relationship with Bernhard now or in the future?

Twelve minutes later

Re:

You're making the wrong assumptions, Leo: I'm not going to fall in love with you!!! It's not going to develop into some romance, affair or passion, whatever you want to call it! We're just going to meet up. As you might meet up with an old friend you haven't seen for a long time. The only tiny difference being that it's not that you haven't seen the friend for a long time, but that you haven't set eyes on him at all. Instead of saying, 'Leo, you haven't changed a bit,' I'd say, 'So that's what you look like, Leo!' That's how it would be.

Eight minutes later

Re:

So you mean you'd be quite happy if it were just *me* who fell in love with *you*, a one-sided thing. Then I'd spend my life sending you red-hot, infatuated, heartbroken e-mails. Followed by poems, songs, maybe even musicals and operas, all full of unrequited passion. And you could tell yourself, Bernhard or both of you, 'You see, it was a good thing I met up with him that time.'

Forty seconds later
Re:

I reckon Marlene's got a lot to answer for!

Four and a half minutes later
Re:

Don't be so evasive, Emmi. Just for once this has absolutely nothing to do with Marlene. It's about the two of us, or the three of us, let's say — you can deny it all you like, but your husband *is* indirectly involved in some kind of way. And I simply don't believe it's coincidental that you want to meet up just now, when you've got your husband at a safe distance in the mountains.

Two minutes later
Re:

You're right, it's not a coincidence. I've got more time to myself this week. Time I'd like to spend with people I'm fond of. Time with friends, or with people who might become friends. Talking of time, it's just after eight and I've got to go. Mia will be waiting. Have a nice evening.

251

Five hours later

Subject: Leo?

Hello Leo, any chance you're still awake? Will you join me for a glass of wine? Leo, Leo, Leo. I'm miserable.

Emmi

Thirteen minutes later

Re:

Yes, I'm still awake. Or rather, I'm awake again. I set my Emmi alarm clock. I've turned the volume of the new mail alert up to full and put the laptop next to my pillow. It just got me out of bed.

I knew you'd write again tonight, Emmi! How late is it, in fact? Ah, I see, just after midnight. You and Mia didn't last very long! (I'm not going to drink any more wine. I've brushed my teeth. And wine after toothpaste is like having noodle soup with your morning coffee.)

Two minutes later

Re:

Leo, I'm soooooo happy you replied!!! How did you know I'd write again tonight?

Seven minutes later
Re:

1) Because you enjoy spending time with people you're fond of. Time 'with friends, or with people who might become friends'.
2) Because you're at home on your own.
3) Because you feel lonely.
4) Because the north wind is blowing.

Two minutes later
Re:

Thank you for not being angry with me, Leo. I've been sending you some horribly mean-spirited e-mails. You're not just any old friend. You mean so much more to me. To me you are. You are. You are. You are someone who answers questions I haven't even asked: yes, I feel lonely, which is why I'm writing to you.

Forty seconds later
Re:

And how was it with Mia?

Two and a half minutes later

Re:

It was ghastly! She doesn't like the way I talk about Bernhard. She doesn't like the way I talk about my marriage. She doesn't like the way I talk about my family. She doesn't like the way I talk about my e-mails. She doesn't like the way I talk about my . . . the way I talk about Leo. She doesn't like the way I talk. She doesn't like the fact that I talk. She doesn't like. She doesn't like me.

One minute later

Re:

But why *did* you talk about all those things? I thought you wanted to go on a pub crawl, like in the good old days.

Three minutes later

Re:

You can't bring back the old days. They're called old for a reason. New days can never be like the old ones. And if you try to make them so, you'll come across as old and jaded, like those people who long for them. We shouldn't always look back to the old days.

Anybody who does is old and backward-looking. Shall I tell you something? I wanted nothing more than to come home — to Leo.

Fifty seconds later

Re:

It's great that I've become your home.

Two minutes later

Re:

Seriously, Leo, what do you think of me and Bernhard, after all Mia and I have told you? Please be honest!

Four minutes later

Re:

Gosh! What sort of question is that for half-past midnight? And anyway, I thought you were trying to keep your 'real life' at a safe distance from me. But since you're asking, I think you have a smoothly functioning marriage.

Forty-five seconds later
Re:

'Smoothly functioning': is that some kind of snide comment? Is there something wrong with that? Why do all my closest friends seem to be telling me that a 'smoothly functioning' relationship is a bad relationship?

Six minutes later
Re:

It wasn't meant to be a snide comment, Emmi. If something functions smoothly it can't be all that bad, can it? It's only bad when it stops functioning smoothly. Then you'd have to ask yourself, 'Why isn't it functioning smoothly any more?' Or, 'Could it possibly function any better?' But I really think I'm the wrong person to talk to about Bernhard and your marriage. Mia's probably the wrong person, too. But Bernhard, yes, I think Bernhard would be the right one.

Thirteen minutes later
Subject: (no subject)
Hey, Emmi, have you gone to sleep?

Thirty-five seconds later
Re:

I really want to hear your voice, Leo.

Twenty-five seconds later
Re:

I'm sorry?

Forty seconds later
Re:

I really want to hear your voice.

Three minutes later
Re:

Do you really? How do you imagine we might do that? Should I make a recording and send it to you? What do you want me to say? Would a microphone test do — 'one, two, three, testing'? Or should I sing a song? (If I happen to hit the right note, I can sustain it and it doesn't sound all that bad.) You could accompany me on the piano . . .

Fifty-five seconds later

Re:

Now, Leo! I REALLY WANT TO HEAR YOUR VOICE NOW. Please grant me this one wish. Call me. 83 17 433. Leave a message on the answerphone. Please, please, please! Just a few words.

One minute later

Re:

And sometime I'd love to hear *you* say those sentences you write in capitals. Do you scream them? Are they ear-piercing? Shrieking?

Two minutes later

Re:

O.K., O.K., I have the following suggestion: you phone me and read one of your e-mails into the answerphone. For example 'Do you really? How do you imagine we might do that? Should I make a recording and send it to you? What do you want me to say? . . . ' etc etc. Then I'll phone you back and say: 'Now, Leo! I REALLY WANT TO HEAR YOUR VOICE NOW. Please grant me this one wish . . . ' and so on.

Three minutes later

Re:

I've got a better idea. Agreed, but let's leave it till tomorrow. I've got to get my voice back in order first. And I'm exhausted. Answerphone session tomorrow evening at 9 o'clock — with a good glass of wine. Is that O.K.?

One minute later

Re:

O.K. Good-rest-of-night, Leo. Thanks for being there. Thanks for having intercepted me. Thanks for existing. Thank you!

Forty-five seconds later

Re:

And now I'm chucking my laptop out of bed! Goodnight.

The following evening

Subject: Our voices

Hi Emmi,

Are we going to go through with this?

Three minutes later

Re:

Definitely. I can't wait.

Two minutes later

Re:

What if you don't like my voice? What if you're shocked? If you think, 'Is that how the guy spoke to me the whole time?' (Cheers! I'm drinking a French *vin de pays*.)

A minute and a half later

Re:

How about the other way round? What if you don't like *my* voice? What if it makes your toes curl? You might not want to talk to me any more. (Chin chin! I'm having a whisky, if that's alright with you. I'm too nervous for wine.)

Two minutes later

Re:

Let's use the two e-mails we've just sent each other. O.K.?

Three minutes later

Re:

But they're quite difficult e-mails, they're mostly questions. When you're talking to someone for the first time, questions are quite hard to say out loud. Particularly for women. Women are at a vocal disadvantage with questions, because their voices have to go up at the end of a sentence, i.e. they're forced up into the higher registers. And if they're nervous as well, they might make gurgling noises. Do you know what I mean? Gurgling sounds stupid.

One minute later

Re:

LET'S START NOW, EMMI! I'll go first. You speak in five minutes. Let's e-mail each other when we've finished. And we won't listen to the answerphone UNTIL AFTER-WARDS. Understood?

Thirty seconds later

Re:

Hang on!!! Your phone number, if you don't mind.

Thirty-five seconds later

Re:

Oh, sorry. 45 20 737. Right, I'm going now.

Nine minutes later

Re:

Done. Your turn!

Seven minutes later

Re:

I'm done. Who's going to listen first?

Fifty seconds later

Re:

Both at the same time.

Forty seconds later

Re:

O.K. And afterwards we'll e-mail each other.

Fourteen minutes later

Re:

Why haven't you written, Leo? If you don't

like my voice, you could at least tell me to my inbox. I think the choice of messages put me, as a woman, at a disadvantage. And that rasping tone isn't me, it's the whisky. And if you don't write to me now I'll finish the whole bottle! And if I get alcohol poisoning I'll send you the hospital bill!

Two minutes later

Re:

Emmi, I'm speechless. I mean, I'm astonished. I imagined you to sound quite different. Tell me, do you always talk like that, or did you disguise your voice?

Forty-five seconds later

Re:

Talk like what?

One minute later

Re:

Unbelievably erotically! Like the presenter of some love and relationships programme.

Seven minutes later

Re:

That sounds alright, I can live with that! You don't sound so bad yourself. The way you talk is much bolder than the way you write. Your voice is really smoky. My favourite bit was 'Is that how the guy spoke to me the whole time?' Especially the words 'guy' and 'spoke'. It's the 'y' in 'guy'. Your 'y' is quite sensational, it's not an 'ai' or a 'ye', in fact it's hardly a sound at all. More of a murmur, a whisper, as if you're exhaling the smoke of a joint through your teeth. I think we underuse the letter 'y', don't you? You should use the 'y' as often as you can. And in 'spoke', it's the 'spo' bit I liked. It's wicked, the way you say it, and damn sexy, like a challenge to . . . well, who cares what, but it's a challenge that you would accept. 'Spo', at least the way you say it, could be the name of a new potency pill. Not Viagra, but Spo, with the voice of Leo Leike — it could be a big hit.

Four minutes later

Re:

What stunned me most of all, Emmi, was how you say the word 'toes'. I've never heard such a graceful, soft, dusky, clear 'toes' before, and I'd never have imagined you would say it like that. No shrieking, no gurgling, no crowing. A really beautiful, soft, elegant, sleek, gentle, tiptoed 'toes'. And 'whisky', that sounded really classy too. The 'wh' like a rope swishing through the air; the 'ky' like a key to your . . . hmm . . . bedroom. (My bottle of wine's almost finished, can you tell?)

One minute later

Re:

Keep drinking, Leo! I love it when you're a bit tiddly. That and hearing your voice turn me on . . .

Twenty minutes later

Re:

Leo? Where are you?

Ten minutes later

Re:

Hang on. I'm just opening another bottle. This French *vin de pays* is good, Emmi! We don't drink French *vin de pays* often enough. Not often enough, and not enough of it. If we drank more *vin de pays* more often, we'd all be happier and we'd sleep better too. Your voice is very erotic, Emmi. I like your voice. Marlene had a very erotic voice, too, but different. Marlene is much colder than you, Emmi. Marlene's voice is deep, but cold. Emmi's voice is deep and warm. And she says, 'whisky, whisky, whisky'. Let's drink one more to us! I'm on French red. I'm going to read all your e-mails again, Emmi, and they'll sound completely different. Until now I've been reading all your e-mails with the wrong voice. I've been reading them all with Marlene's voice. For me, Emmi was Marlene, Marlene at the very beginning, when everything was still possible. All there was was love — nothing else. Everything was possible. How are you, Emmi?

Five minutes later

Re:

Oh no! Do you have to drink so fast, Leo? Can't you hang on a bit longer? If your head's already hit the keyboard I'll just say goodnight, my friend. It's wonderful being with you. Wonderful, but sometimes — and especially when it's just getting interesting — distinctly short (mainly because of alcohol). Ah well, at least I have the answerphone message. Before I go to bed I'll treat myself to a few more rounds of Leo Leike's 'Is that how the guy spoke to me the whole time?' I'm sure it will help against the north wind.

Twelve minutes later

Re:

Don't go to bed yet, Emmi! I'm still awake, I'm feeling fine. Come to me, Emmi! Let's have another drink. Whisper 'whisky, whisky, whisky' into my ear. Say 'toes'. Show them to me. I'll say, 'So those are the famous Emmi toes of the famous Emmi feet with the famous size 37 shoes. I'll only put my hand on your shoulder, I promise. Just a hug. Just a kiss. Just a few kisses, nothing more. Totally harmless kisses. Emmi, I have to know what you smell like. I've got your voice in my ears, now I need your smell in my nose. I'm being serious, Emmi. Come over to my place. I'll pay for the taxi. No, you don't want me to do that. Who cares who pays for the taxi? Hochleitnergasse 17, flat 15. Come over! Or do you want me to come to your place? I could come over to yours! Just a sniff. Just a kiss. No sex. You're married — unfortunately.

267

No sex, I promise. Bernhard, I promise! I just want to smell your skin, Emmi. I really don't want to know what you look like. We won't turn the lights on. Total darkness. Just a few kisses, Emmi. Is that so awful? Is that cheating? What is cheating? An e-mail? Or a voice? Or a sniff? Or a kiss? I want to be with you now. I want to have my arms around you. Just one night together with Emmi. I'll close my eyes. I don't have to know what you look like. I just need to smell, kiss and feel you, very close. I'm laughing with happiness. Is that cheating, Emmi?

Five minutes later
Re:

'Is that how the guy spoke to me the whole time?' Night night, Leo. It's good to be with you. Astonishingly good. Amazingly good!!! I could get used to it. I have got used to it.

8

The following morning

Subject: (no subject)

Good morning, Leo. Bad news. I've got to go to the South Tirol. Bernhard's in hospital. The doctors think it was some kind of heatstroke. I've got to drive down and fetch the kids. I've got a headache (too much whisky!). Thanks for a lovely evening. I don't know what 'cheating' is either. All I know is that I need you, Leo, I need you very badly. And I need my family too. I'm off now. I'll be in touch again tomorrow. I hope you feel O.K. after all that French stuff . . .

The following day

Subject: Everything O.K.?

Why no message from Leo? I just wanted to let you know that we're back, and Bernhard was able to come home too. It was a circulatory collapse, but he's back on his feet already. Please e-mail me!!

Two hours later

Subject: To Mr Leike

Dear Mr Leike,

I have found it very hard to write you this message. I'll admit I'm embarrassed, and the embarrassment I'm bringing upon myself increases with every line. My name is Bernhard Rothner — I believe I don't need to give you more of an introduction. Mr Leike, I have a huge favour to ask of you. When I tell you what this favour is you will be amazed, possibly even shocked. I will then try to explain my motives for asking this favour. I am no great writer, regrettably, and I'm not really familiar with e-mail. But I will endeavour to say all those things that have been concerning me for months, things which have put my life out of joint, my life and that of my family, even my wife's, and I believe I can judge this accurately after so many harmonious years of marriage.

And so to the favour: Mr Leike, meet my wife! Please do it, finally, and bring this nightmare to an end! We're grown men, I can't dictate what you do. I can only implore you: meet her! I'm feeling inferior and powerless, and suffering because of it. How humiliating do you think it is for me to write such lines as these? You, on the other hand, haven't shown the slightest weakness, Mr Leike. You have nothing to reproach yourself for. And me, I don't have anything to reproach you for either, unfortunately. I really don't. You can't reproach a mind. You're not palpable, Mr Leike, you're not tangible. You're not real. You're just my wife's fantasy, an illusion of unlimited emotional happiness, an other-worldly rapture, a utopia of love, but all fashioned out of words. Against this I'm impotent; all I can do is wait until fate is merciful and turns you at last into a creature of flesh and blood, a man with contours, with strengths and weaknesses, something to aim at. Only when my wife can see you as she sees me, as someone vulnerable, an imperfect being, an example of that flawed construct which is man; only when you have met face to face will your superiority vanish. Only then can I compete with you on an equal footing, Mr Leike. Only then can I fight for Emma.

My wife once wrote to you, 'Leo, please don't force me to open my family album.' But now I find myself obliged to do it in her stead. When we met, Emma was twenty-three and I was her piano teacher at the Academy of Music, fourteen years her senior, happily married and the father of two delightful children. A car accident destroyed our family — our three-year-old was traumatized, the elder one badly injured. I suffered permanent injuries, and the children's mother, my wife Johanna, died. Without the piano I would have fallen apart. But music when it's played is life itself — nothing can remain dead for ever. If you're a musician and you play music, you live out memories as if they were happening now. Music helped me pull myself back together. And then there were my pupils, there was a distraction, there was a job to do, there was meaning. And then, out of the blue, there was Emma. This lively, sparkling, sassy, gorgeous young woman began — all by herself — to pick up the pieces of our life, without expecting anything in return. Extraordinary people like her are put on to this earth to counter sadness. They are few and far between. I don't know how I deserved it, but suddenly she was there by my side. The children ran straight to her, and I fell head over heels in love with her.

What about her? Mr Leike, I bet you're wondering, 'But what about Emma?' Did she, this 23-year-old student, fall equally in love with this sorrowful old knight, soon to be forty, who was being kept together by little more than keys and notes? I can't answer this question, not to you, nor even to myself. How much was it down to her admiration for my music? (I was very successful at the time, an acclaimed pianist.) How much was pity, sympathy, a desire to help, the capacity to be there through the bad times? How much did I remind her of her father, who left her when she was very young? How much of it was her doting on my sweet Fiona and little, golden Jonas? To what extent was it my own euphoria reflected in her, to what extent did she love my boundless love for her, rather than love me? How much did she relish the certainty that I would never be unfaithful, a guaranteed lifetime of dependability, the assurance of my eternal loyalty? Please believe me, Mr Leike, I would never have dared get close to her if I had not felt that her feelings for me were as strong as mine for her. It was obvious that she felt drawn to me and the children; she wanted to be part of our world, an influential part, a definitive part, the heart of it. Two years later we got married. That was eight years ago. (I'm sorry, I've just ruined your game of hide-and-seek: the 'Emmi' you know is thirty-four years young.) Not a day passed without my astonishment at having this vital young beauty at my side. And every day I waited in trepidation for 'it' to happen, for a younger man to appear, one of the many who have admired and idolized her. And Emma would say, 'Bernhard, I've fallen in love with somebody else. Where do we go from here?' This nightmare has failed to materialize. A far worse one has come to pass. You, Mr Leike, the silent 'other world'. Illusions of love via e-mail, feelings intensifying day by day, a growing yearning, unsated passion, everything directed towards one apparently real goal, an ultimate goal which is forever being postponed, the meeting of all meetings, but one which will never take place because it would dispel the artifice of ultimate happiness, total satisfaction, without end, with no expiry date, which can be lived only in the mind. Against that I'm impotent.

Mr Leike, since you 'arrived', as it were, it's as though Emmi is transformed. She's absent-minded and distanced from me. She sits in her room for hours on end, staring at the computer screen, into the cosmos of her dreams. She lives in her 'other world', she lives with it. When there's a beatific smile on her face, it's no longer for me — it hasn't been for a long time. She has to make a real effort to hide her distraction from the children. I can see just what a torture it is for her to sit next to me now. Do you know how much that hurts? I've tried to ride out this phase by being extremely tolerant. I've never wanted Emma to feel constrained by me. Neither of us has ever been jealous. But all of a sudden I no longer knew what to do. I mean, there was nothing and nobody there, no actual person, no obvious interloper — until I discovered the root of the problem. I could have died with shame that the whole thing had gone as far as it has. I snooped around in Emma's room. Eventually, in a secret drawer, I found a folder, a fat folder full of documents: her entire e-mail correspondence with a certain Leo Leike, printed out nice and crisp, page by page, message by message. I copied these documents with a trembling hand, and for a few weeks I managed to put them out of my mind. We had a ghastly holiday in Portugal. The little one was ill, the older one fell madly in love with a sports instructor. My wife and I didn't say a word to each other for a fortnight, but both of us tried to fool the other that everything was just fine, as it always was, as it always had to be. After that I could hold out no longer. I took the folder with me on the walking holiday, and in a fit of self-destruction, out of some masochistic desire to make myself suffer, I read through all the e-mails in one night. Let me tell you, since the death of my first wife I have experienced no greater emotional torture. When I had finished reading I couldn't get out of bed. My daughter phoned the emergency services and I was taken to hospital. My wife collected me the day before yesterday. Now you know the whole story.

Mr Leike, please meet Emma! And now I come to the wretched nadir of my self-humiliation. Meet her, spend a night with her, have sex with her! I know that you'll want to. I'll 'allow' you to. I'm giving you *carte blanche*, I'm absolving you of all scruples, I won't think of it as infidelity. I sense that Emma wants physical as well as mental intimacy with you, she wants to 'know' it, thinks she needs it, something's urging her to do it. That's the thrill, the novelty, the variety I cannot offer her. So many men have worshipped and lusted after Emma, but it never struck me that she felt attracted to any of them. And then I saw the e-mails she has written to you. Suddenly I understood just how great her desire can be if aroused by the 'right one'. You, Mr Leike, are her chosen one. And I'm almost wishing you would sleep with her once. ONCE (like my wife I'm using emphatic block capitals). ONCE. JUST ONCE! Let that be the culmination of the passion you have built up in writing. Make that the conclusion. Crown your e-mail correspondence, and put a stop to it. Give me back my wife, you unearthly, untouchable being! Release her. Bring her back down to earth. Let our family continue to live. Don't do it as a favour to me or my children. Do it for Emma, for her sake. I beg you!

And now I come to the end of my embarrassing, distressing *cri de coeur*, my excruciating appeal for mercy. Just one final request, Mr Leike. Don't betray my confidence. Leave me outside your shared narrative. I have abused Emma's trust, I have gone behind her back, I have read her private, intimate correspondence. I have atoned for this. I could never look her in the eye again if she knew I had been spying. She could never look me in the eye again if she knew what I had read. She would hate both herself and me in equal measure. Please, Mr Leike, spare us that. Don't tell her about this letter. Once more, I beg you!

So now I'm going to send the most excruciating letter I have ever written.

Yours sincerely,

Bernhard Rothner

Four hours later

Re:

Dear Mr Rothner,

I got your e-mail. I don't know what to say. I don't even know if I should say anything. I'm shocked. You haven't just humiliated yourself, you've shamed all three of us. I need to think. I'm going to draw back for a while. I can't promise you anything, I can't promise anything at all.

Kind regards,

Leo Leike

The following day

Subject: Leo???

Leo, where are you? I can't stop hearing your voice. Always saying the same thing: 'Is that how the guy spoke to me the whole time?' I know exactly how the guy speaks. The only problem is, he hasn't spoken for days. Did you down too much *vin de pays* that night? Can you even remember? You invited me to Hochleitnergasse 17, Flat 15. 'Just a sniff', you wrote. You have no idea how close I was to coming over. Closer than I've ever been. You occupy my thoughts twenty-four hours a day. Why won't you write to me? Should I be worried?

The following day
Subject: Leo??????
Leo, what's wrong? Please write to me!
Your Emmi

Half an hour later
Subject: To Mr Rothner

Dear Mr Rothner,

Let me propose a little deal. You have to promise me something. And I'll promise you something in return. So, I promise that I won't say a word to your wife about your email and how it came about. And you have to promise me that you will NEVER AGAIN READ A SINGLE E-MAIL that your wife writes to me, or I to her. I trust you not to break that promise, if you agree to it, that is. And you too can be assured that I'll be as good as my word. If you agree, please say so. Otherwise I'll tell your wife the secrets you were good enough to share with me.

Regards,
Leo Leike

Two hours later

Re:

Yes, Mr Leike, I promise. I will no longer read any e-mails not addressed to me. I've already read too many things I shouldn't have. And now may I reiterate my request: Will you meet my wife?

Ten minutes later

Re:

Mr Rothner,

I can't answer that. And even if I could, I wouldn't. In writing to me I think you made a grave error, symptomatic of a blatant flaw in your marriage. It's probably been there for years. You wrote to the wrong address. You should have told your wife everything you've said to me, but much sooner, right at the beginning. I think you should be doing that right now! Make up for it! And please don't send me any more e-mails. I believe you've said everything you thought you needed to. That was already too much.

Kind regards,

Leo Leike

Fifteen minutes later

Subject: (no subject)

Hi Emmi,

Just back from a work trip to Cologne. Sorry, it was so frantic I didn't even have a few minutes to write to you in peace. I hope your family is in better health now. I'm going to take advantage of this nice weather and go away for a few days, somewhere south, where no-one can get hold of me. I think it's what I need — I'm feeling pretty drained. I'll write when I'm back. Enjoy these lovely sunny days. I hope dislocated arms are kept to a minimum.

Lots and lots of love,

Leo

Five minutes later

Re:

What's her name?

Ten minutes later

Re:

What's whose name?

Four minutes later

Re:

Please don't insult my intelligence, Leo, or my Leo-sensor. Whenever you start blustering about frantic work trips and having to make the most of the good weather, or whingeing about being drained, or warning me in advance that you'll be out of contact, or even ordering me to enjoy the sunny days ahead, there's only one thing I can put it down to. What's her name? Could it possibly be — Marlene?

Eight minutes later

Re:

No Emmi, you've got it all wrong. There's no Marlene, nor anybody else. I just need to get away. The last few weeks and months have worn me out. I need a break.

One minute later

Re:

A break from me?

Five minutes later

Re:

A break from myself! I'll write again in a few days. Promise!

Three days later

Subject: Missing Leo!

Hi Leo, it's me. I know you're not there, you're having a break from yourself just now. How does one actually do that? I wish I could. I urgently need a break from myself, but instead I'm fully occupied with me. And it's exhausting. I have to admit something, Leo. Actually I don't *have* to admit it, and it's not a good thing that I am, but I can't help it. Leo, I'm so unhappy at the moment. And do you know why? (You probably don't want to know at all, but that's just too bad — sorry.) Because you're not there. E-mails from Leo make me happy. And I'm unhappy because I'm not getting them. It is my misfortune that my happiness depends so much on your e-mails. And now that I know your voice, I'm missing your e-mails three times as much.

I was with Mia yesterday evening and late into the night. It was the best time we'd had together for years. And do you know why? (This is mean, I know, but you have to hear it.) It was our best time together because at long last I was unhappy. Mia said I seemed the same as ever, the only difference being that this time I admitted I was unhappy, to myself as well as to her. And for that she's grateful. Sounds pretty sad, doesn't it?

Mia thinks that I've fallen in love with you in a peculiar way — through words. She says I can't live without you at the moment, at least not happily. And she says she can understand why. Awful, isn't it? But I love my husband too. I honestly do. I chose him, him and his children, him and my children. I wanted this family and no other, and I still do. At the time it was a tragic situation, I'll tell you about it one day. (Have you noticed I'm talking about my family without you even asking . . .) Bernhard has never let me down, and he never will. He gives me all the freedom I want, and he responds to my every need. He's a very educated, unselfish, calm, lovely man. You can feel suffocated by routine over time, of course. Sometimes things are too ordered; there aren't enough surprises. We know each other inside out, and we have no more secrets from each other. Mia said, 'Perhaps what you're after is the secrecy of it all. Perhaps you've fallen in love with a hot secret.' So I said, 'What should I do? I can't suddenly turn

Bernhard into a hot secret too.' What do *you* think, Leo? Can I turn Bernhard into a hot secret? Can I make a hot secret out of eight years of family life?

Oh Leo, Leo, Leo. Everything's *so hard* at the moment. I'm in a bad place. I've got no drive. I've got no passion. I've got no — Leo, the one and only Leo. I don't know where all this is going. I don't want to know. I don't even care. The main thing is that you write to me again soon. Please hurry up with your break from yourself. I want to drink wine with you again. I want you to want to kiss me again. (Was that a proper sentence?) I don't need real kisses. I need the man who's sometimes so desperate to kiss me that he has to write to tell me so. I need Leo. I feel so lonely with my whisky bottle. I've had so much whisky, Leo, have you noticed? How would it be, a life together with you? Would you still be desperate to kiss me after weeks, months, years — or would it last for ever? I know I shouldn't be thinking like this. I'm happily married. But at the same time I feel unhappy. I'm probably contradicting myself. You're the contradiction, Leo. Thanks for listening. Just one more whisky. Goodnight, Leo. I miss you so much. I would even kiss you blindfold. I really would. Right now.

Two days later

Subject: Not a word

Thirty degrees, and not a word from the man on a break from himself. I realize that my e-mail from a couple of days ago was verging on the painful. Was it too much for you, Leo? Believe me, it was the whisky! The whisky and me. What's deep inside me and what the whisky dragged out.

Longingly,

Emmi

The following day

Subject: (no subject)

A southerly wind — and still I'm tossing and turning in bed. A single syllable from you would send me straight to sleep. Goodnight, dear man-on-a-break-from-himself.

Two days later

Subject: My last message

This is the last e-mail I'm going to send without hearing back. What you're doing to me is so harsh, Leo! Please stop, because it's hurting like hell. You can do anything you want, anything except keep up this silence.

The next day

Subject: Counter-message

Dear Emmi,

It only took me a few hours to make a life-changing decision. But it's taken me nine days to tell you the consequences. In a few weeks' time I'll be moving to Boston for at least two years. I'm going to be running a project group at a university there. The job is extremely attractive, both academically and financially. My circumstances permit me this spontaneity — there are only a few things here I'd have to give up. Moving halfway across the world must be in the blood. I'll miss a few close friends. I'll miss my sister Adrienne. And I'll miss . . . Emmi. Yes, I'll miss her particularly.

I've also made another decision. It sounds so harsh that my fingers are trembling in anticipation of having to tell you. O.K., here it comes, after this colon: I'm going to stop our e-mail contact. I have to get you out of my head, Emmi. It can't be that you're the first and last thought I have each day for the rest of my life. That's sick. You're 'spoken for', you have a family, you have duties, challenges, responsibilities. You're very attached to all that, and it's the world you're happy in. This you've made perfectly clear. (With a heady cocktail of whisky and longing it's possible to write oneself into an unhappy mood, as you did in your last long e-mail, but the very next morning it's gone.) I'm certain your husband loves you, as only someone who's spent so many years living together with a woman can. Perhaps all you're missing is a touch of extra-marital adventure playing out in your head, something cosmetic to brighten up your day-to-day emotional life. That's why you're so attached to me. That's what keeps our written relationship going. But instead of enriching your life in the long run I suspect it just creates more confusion.

Now, about me. I'm thirty-six years old (so now you know). I don't intend to spend my life with a woman who is only mine in my inbox. Boston will be a fresh start. All of a sudden I have this desire to meet a woman in a frightfully conventional way again. First I'll see her, then I'll hear her voice, then I'll smell her, then maybe I'll kiss her. The backwards path we took was — and is — extremely exciting, but it doesn't lead anywhere. I've got to get rid of this mental block. For months now I've seen Emmi in every beautiful woman in the street. But none of them has been able to measure up to the real one, none of them has been able to compete. Because I've hidden my real Emmi far from public view. I've cut her off, isolated her, and kept her all for myself — in my computer. And that's where she's met me after work. She's waited for me there before, after or instead of breakfast. She's wished me goodnight after a long evening together. Often she's stayed up with me until dawn, beside me, in my room, in my bed, secretly tucked under the covers. But the truth is she has remained unattainable in every phase of our relationship. The images I have of her are so delicate and frail that had I seen her in the flesh, they would surely have cracked and broken. This artificially generated Emmi has seemed to me so fragile that she would have shattered if I'd ever actually touched her. Physically she's been nothing more than the air between the computer keys which I've used to create her day by day. One puff and she would have been gone. Yes, that's what it's come to, Emmi. I'm going to close my inbox, I'm going to puff at my keyboard, I'm going to put the screen down. I'm going to say goodbye.

Yours,

Leo

The following day

Subject: You call that a goodbye?

Was that your final e-mail? I can't believe it! I hereby lose all faith in final e-mails. I mean, Leo, hell-O-O! If you want to just disappear, I'm not expecting some kind of comic *tour de force*. But what the hell was that, a tragic farce? That's no goodbye! How do you want me to picture you as you melodramatically blow at your keyboard? O.K., fair enough, I've been letting myself go a little. And I've started to drone on a bit. My bubbly disposition has sometimes been as heavy as a sack of cement. Yup, I've been carrying around the cumbersome baggage of our electronic mail. I've fallen just a little bit in love with Mister Anonymous, it has to be said. Neither of us has been able to get the other quite out of our head — I think we're both guilty here. But that's no reason for us go on as if we're some kind of virtual Tristan and Isolde.

Off you go to Boston, then. Sever e-mail contact with me if you like. But don't finish it like that!! That's beneath you, both stylistically and emotionally, and it's way beneath my dignity, dear friend. Puffing on the keyboard? For God's sake, Leo! What a load of crap! It makes me wonder, 'Is that how the guy spoke to me the whole time?'

Please prove to me that wasn't your last e-mail. I'd rather have something more upbeat, something surprising, a finish with a flourish, a good punchline. How about: 'To round things off, I suggest we meet up!' At least that would be a funny ending. (And now, if you don't mind, I'm going to go and have a good cry.)

Five hours later
Re:
Dear Emmi,
To round things off I suggest we meet up!

Five minutes later
Re:
You're not serious?

One minute later
Re:
Oh yes I am. I wouldn't joke about that, Emmi.

Two minutes later
Re:

What am I supposed to make of that? Is that a whim? Is it because I gave you the right cue? Have I turned you from a melodramatist into a satirist?

Three minutes later
Re:

No, Emmi, it's not a whim, it's a well-thought-out proposition. You just pre-empted me. Let me say it again. I'd like to conclude our e-mail relationship with a meeting. One single encounter before I move to Boston.

Fifty seconds later
Re:

One single encounter? What do you hope to gain from that?

Three minutes later
Re:

Insight. Relief. Catharsis. Clarity. Friendship. The solution to a personality puzzle which I created and then blew out of all proportion. A removal of barriers. Feeling good afterwards. The best antidote to the north wind. A conclusion befitting this exciting phase in our lives. The simple answer to thousands of complicated, unresolved questions. Or, as you said yourself, 'At least that would be a funny ending.'

Five minutes later
Re:

I have a feeling it might not be at all funny.

Forty-five seconds later
Re:

That depends on us.

Two minutes later
Re:

On us? You're on your own there, Leo. I haven't agreed to a last-minute meeting at all, and quite frankly I'm a long way off doing so right now. First I'd like to know a bit more about this 'first date/last date' meeting. Where do you want to meet?

Fifty-five seconds later
Re:
Wherever you like, Emmi.

Forty-five seconds later
Re:
And what will we do?

Forty seconds later
Re:
Whatever we want.

Thirty-five seconds later
Re:
What do we want?

Thirty seconds later
Re:
That remains to be seen.

Three minutes later
Re:
I think I'd rather get e-mails from Boston.
Then we don't have to wait and see whether

either of us wants anything. At least I know that I want something, and I know what it is: e-mails from Boston.

One minute later

Re:

Emmi, I'm not going to write you e-mails from Boston. I'd like to stop it, really I would. I'm convinced it would be the best thing for both of us.

Fifty seconds later

Re:

Then how long do you intend to keep on e-mailing me for?

Two minutes later

Re:

Until we meet. Unless you say you definitely don't want to. Then this would be a kind of final sentence.

One minute later

Re:

That's blackmail, Maestro! You can put things pretty crudely sometimes: just read your last e-mail. I'm not sure I want to meet somebody who writes things like that. Goodnight.

The following morning
Subject: (no subject)

Good morning, Leo! I'm DEFINITELY NOT going to meet you in Café Huber.

One hour later
Re:

We don't have to. But why not?

One minute later
Re:

Because it's the kind of place you meet workmates or chance acquaintances.

Two minutes later
Re:

Chance acquaintances? Who could possibly better qualify for that than us?

Fifty seconds later

Re:

Is this the attitude you've maintained throughout our correspondence, beginning, middle and end? If so, I suggest we don't have this chance, ephemeral meeting.

The following day

Subject: (no subject)

What exactly is the matter with you, Leo? Why are your e-mails so boorish and obstructive all of a sudden? Why are you disparaging 'our story'? Are you *trying* to be insensitive and vicious? Is this an attempt to make your exit easier to bear?

Two and a half hours later

Re:

I'm sorry, Emmi, I'm at my wits' end trying to get 'our story' out of my head. I've already explained why I need to do it. I realise that since 'Boston' my e-mails have sounded horribly impersonal. I hate writing like this, but I'm forcing myself to. I don't want to invest any more emotion into 'our story'. I don't want to continue building things up before I let it all tumble down. All I really want now is this meeting. I think it would do us both good.

Two minutes later
Re:

And what happens if we want to meet a second time?

Four minutes later
Re:

As far as I'm concerned that's not a possibility. I mean, I've already excluded it as a possibility. I want to meet just this once, to give 'our story' the ending it deserves before I leave for America.

Fifteen minutes later
Re:

And what would you consider that to be? Or to put another way, how would you like me to remember you after we've met:

1) Quite nice, but not nearly as interesting as in his e-mails. Now I can perfectly happily delete him from every aspect of my life with a good conscience.

2) I can't believe I've spent a year with this bore.

3) The perfect man to have an affair with. Shame he's going to be living on the other side of the Atlantic.

4) He's drop-dead gorgeous! What an intoxicating evening! Really worth all those months of e-mailing. Now that that's ticked off, I can concentrate on making Jonas' packed lunch.

5) Shit! He's the one. I'd have dumped Bernhard and given up my family for him. But now he's escaping to America, the land of no e-mails. But I shall wait for him! I shall light a candle for him every day. And I shall include him in my prayers — after the one for the children — until he returns in all his glory and splendour . . .

Three minutes later
Re:
I'm going to miss your sarcasm, Emmi.

Two minutes later
Re:
You can take a whole heap of it to Boston

with you, if you like. I have plenty to spare. So: which of these men would you most like to be after our official parting?

Five minutes later

Re:

I'm not going to be any of them. I'm going to be who I am. And you'll see me as I am. At least you'll see me as you think I am. Or see me as who you want to think I am.

One minute later

Re:

Will I want to meet you again?

Forty-five seconds later

Re:

No.

Thirty-five seconds later

Re:

Why not?

Fifty seconds later
Re:
Because that won't be possible.

One minute later
Re:
Everything's possible.

Forty seconds later
Re:
Except that. Because it's impossible, full stop.

Fifty-five seconds later
Re:
Things which seem impossible beforehand often turn out to be possible after all. And sometimes they're not the worst.

Two minutes later
Re:
I'm sorry, Emmi. There is no possibility that we'll meet again. You'll see.

One minute later

Re:

Why would I want to? If I know that there'll be no second meeting, why would I want to come to a first?

Two minutes later

Subject: To Mr Leike

Dear Mr Leike,

We're going through a torrid time. If this doesn't stop, our marriage is going to collapse. I can't imagine that this is your intention. Please, meet my wife and stop writing to her (I swear I have no idea what you're writing to each other, nor do I want to know any more. I just want it to stop once and for all).

With kind regards,

Bernhard Rothner

Three minutes later

Re:

You yourself have to know why you want to meet me, Emmi — if you do want to. All I can say is that I definitely want to meet you! I think by now I've explained why. Have a nice evening,

Love,

Leo

One minute later

Re:

Icy Leo Leike. 'Is that how the guy spoke to me the whole time.' Pretty sad, really.

9

Three days later

Subject: Questions outstanding

Hi Leo,

It seems you're not e-mailing me any more. Are you going to answer my e-mails at all? How long for? When are you going to Boston?

Kind regards,

Emmi

Nine hours later

Re:

Good evening, Emmi. I'm afraid my life is a mess. I'm bang in the middle of preparations for the move to America. My flight's on 16 July, so a fortnight tomorrow. So I'll say it once more: it would be great if we could meet before I go. If you're not sure whether you want to, just do it for my sake, please. I really want to! It would make me so happy if you said yes. I know I'd feel better afterwards. And I'm sure you'd feel good too.

Twelve minutes later

Re:

Don't you understand, Leo? As it's supposed to be a 'farewell meeting', I'll only feel good afterwards if it turns out that you're different from the man who's been writing to me for an entire year (apart from some of your ghastly, impersonal messages of late). If you *are* 'different', our meeting would be a huge disappointment, and the only good thing about it would be that it's our last. So if you're convinced I would feel good afterwards, then you're telling me *indirectly* that the meeting would be a disappointment. And so I'll ask you again: Why should I agree to a meeting which can only be a disappointment?

Eight minutes later

Re:

I don't think our meeting would have to be disappointing for you to feel better than . . . you do today, for example.

One minute later

Re:

Today? How do you know how I feel today?

Fifty seconds later
Re:
You're not on good form today, Emmi.

Thirty seconds later
Re:
And what about you?

Thirty-five seconds later
Re:
I'm not on great form either.

Twenty-five seconds later
Re:
Why not?

Forty-five seconds later
Re:
For the same reason that you're not.

Fifty seconds later
Re:
But you're to blame, Leo. No-one's forcing you to disappear from my life.

Forty seconds later
Re:
But they are!

Forty seconds later
Re:
Who is?

The following morning
Subject: I am!
I am!
I'm forcing myself. Me, and reason.

An hour and a half later
Re:
So who is it that wants to meet up with me?
Is that you plus reason? Or you plus
unreason? Or mere unreason? Or (the worst
option) sheer reason?

Twenty minutes later
Re:
Me, my reason, my emotions, my hands, my
feet, my eyes, my nose, my ears, my mouth.

Every bit of me wants to meet you, Emmi.

Three minutes later
Re:
Your mouth?

Fifteen minutes later
Re:
Yes, of course: to talk.

Fifty seconds later
Re:
I see.

Two days later
Subject: O.K.
Hi Leo,
As far as I'm concerned, we might as well risk it. Let's meet up, what difference would it make? When are you free this week?

An hour and a half later

Re:

I'll let you decide. Wednesday, Thursday, Friday?

One minute later

Re:

Tomorrow

Three minutes later

Re:

Tomorrow? Fine, tomorrow. Morning, lunch-time, afternoon, evening?

One minute later

Re:

Evening. Where, though?

Ten minutes later

Re:

At a café of your choice. At a restaurant of your choice. At a museum of your choice. On a walk of your choice. On a park bench of your choice. On a chair of your choice. Or in any other place of your choice.

Fifty seconds later

Re:

At your place.

Eight minutes later

Re:

Why?

Forty seconds later

Re:

Why not?

One minute later

Re:

What do you have in mind?

Fifty-five seconds later

Re:

What do *you* have in mind, Leo? You're the one wanting this farewell meeting, may I remind you.

Thirty-five minutes later

Re:

I've got nothing at all in mind. I just want to see the woman who's been with me for months, who's made a mark on my life. I want to hear more of her lovely voice, more than 'whisky' and 'toes'. I want to watch her lips as she says, 'What do *you* have in mind, Leo? You're the one who wanted this farewell meeting, may I remind you.' How do the corners of her mouth move, how do her eyes shine, how do her eyebrows rise when she utters sentences like these? What expression does she have when she's being ironic? What traces have the years of nightly north wind left on her cheeks? Hundreds of things like these interest me about Emmi.

Five minutes later

Re:

Your interest comes a little late, Leo. One evening might not be long enough for this kind of physiognomical research. How many hours were you planning for? How long should I stay?

311

Three minutes later

Re:

For as long as we both want.

One minute later

Re:

And if we don't agree?

Four minutes later

Re:

Then I suppose we'll go with whoever wants to finish first.

Fifty seconds later

Re:

Which will probably be you.

Forty seconds later

Re:

That's not certain.

Twenty minutes later

Re:

It's astonishing how little is certain, despite the fact we're writing to each other all the time. How will we greet each other, for example? Will we shake hands? Clap each other on the shoulders? Should I extend the slender fingers of an elegant hand for you to kiss? Should I proffer one of my cheeks, weathered by the north wind? Will you approach me mouth first? Or will we just stare at each other for a while, like aliens?

Three minutes later

Re:

I suggest I put a glass of wine in your hand and we'll propose a toast. To us.

Two minutes later

Re:

Have you got any whisky? And I don't mean a manky old bottle with three millimetres of some algaefied yellowy-brown liquid at the bottom. In that case *I'll* be the one who decides when we finish, and it'll be a very short meeting indeed.

One minute later

Re:

It's not the whisky that will scupper our meeting.

Forty-five seconds later

Re:

What will, then?

Two minutes later

Re:

Nothing. It'll be a lovely, lively, harmless and enjoyable meeting, Emmi, you'll see.

Three hours later

Re:

Do you have a moment, Leo? I know it's late, but pour yourself another glass of wine — it always does you the world of good. Thing is, I can't stop thinking about everything and I've got a few questions. On my special subject, for example:

1) Do you think you might want to sleep with me at our farewell meeting?

2) Do you think I might want to sleep with you?

3) If the answer to both of the above is yes (and if we actually do sleep together): do you really believe that we'll feel good afterwards? You know, the way you promised me: 'And I'm sure you'd feel good too.'

4) How does that tie in with your prediction that I won't want to meet you again?

Ten minutes later

Re:

1) I think I might want to sleep with you, but I don't have to show it.

2) I think you *might* want to sleep with me, but probably not.

3) Would we feel good afterwards? Yes, I think we would.

4) You won't want to meet me again because you have a family, and after our meeting you'll know exactly where you belong.

Seven minutes later
Re:

1) If you wanted to sleep with me, do you really think I wouldn't notice?
2) And as for whether *I* might want to sleep with you: you're not far off when you say 'probably not'. (Just so you don't get your hopes up.)
3) Would we feel good afterwards? I like it when you talk like a normal man for a change — it sounds so down to earth.
4) You think I'll know exactly where I belong: do you really think at this stage you can judge that better than I can?
5) And one last question before we go to bed, Leo: Are you still just a little bit in love with me?

One minute later
Re:
A little bit?

Two minutes later
Re:
Goodnight. I'm very much in love with you.

I'm terrified of our meeting. I can't imagine
— I can hardly bear to imagine — that then
I'm going to lose you.

All my love,

Emmi

Three minutes later

Re:

You should never think about 'losing'. You
lose just by thinking about it. Goodnight, my
love.

The following morning

Subject: (no subject)

Good morning, Leo. I didn't sleep a wink.
Should I really come over to your place this
evening?

Five minutes later

Re:

Good morning, Emmi. I'm glad I'm not the
only one who didn't sleep. Yes, do come over.
Is 7 o'clock O.K.? We could sit out on the
terrace for a while.

Two hours later

Re:

Leo, Leo, Leo, let's assume this evening goes better than you think. Let's assume you fall in love with the woman you see before you, with the expression that goes with her irony, with the sound of her voice, with her hand movements, with her eyes, her hair (I'm not going to mention her breasts), with her right earlobe, with her left shinbone, whatever. Let's assume you feel there's more that connects us than our computer servers, and that it's not mere coincidence that we've become so caught up in each other. Do you think you might not want to see me again, Leo? Might you not want to keep on writing to me, even from Boston? Might you not want to be together with me? Might you not want to stay together with me? Might you not want to live with me?

Ten minutes later

Re:

EMMI YOU ARE NOT FREE FOR A LIFE TOGETHER WITH ME.

Thirty-five minutes later

Re:

Let's assume I was.

Forty-five minutes later

Subject: (no subject)

Leeeooo, can't you think of anything to say?

Three minutes later

Re:

Dear Emmi,

Let's assume that's just one assumption too many. Let's assume I can't assume that you're free, for the simple reason that you're not, nor will you be. If you 'make yourself free' from your family for the evening — for my sake — then so much the better for me (and for you too, I hope). But that's very different from saying that you're free for me. Generally I'm pretty good at assuming assumptions. But with the best will in the world I can't assume this assumption, however alluring it may sound.

May I take this opportunity to ask you a question? — I know you don't like questions like this, but it's fairly relevant: What are you actually going to tell your husband about where you're going tonight?

Nine minutes later

Re:

Oh, Leo, can't you give it a rest? I'll tell him I'm meeting up with a friend. He'll ask: Do I know him? I'll reply: I don't think so, I haven't told you much about him. Then I'll say: We've got lots to catch up on so I might be late home. He'll say: Have fun.

Twenty minutes later

Re:

And what if you don't get home until the small hours? What will he say then?

Three minutes later

Re:

Do you really think I might get home that late? This is a side to Leo I haven't come across before.

Eight minutes later

Re:

What does Emmi Rothner say? 'Things which seem impossible beforehand often turn out to be possible after all.' In short, everything's possible. I'm beginning to believe that too.

Four minutes later

Re:

Wow, exciting! I like it when you talk like that. (Maybe because those are my words.) Only four hours to go, by the way. Would you like to know which of the three Emmis from the café you'll be opening the door to?

Three minutes later

Re:

No, don't tell me, Emmi! I really *don't* want to know. Let me make a suggestion. You're not allowed to laugh, I'm being serious. I'd like to leave the door ajar. You come in. You go into the first room on the left from the hall. It's dark. I put my arms around you without seeing you. I kiss you blind. One kiss. Just a single kiss!

Fifty seconds later

Re:

And then I leave, or what?

Three minutes later

Re:

No, not at all! One kiss, and then we'll put the blinds up, then we'll see who we've kissed. Then I'll give you a glass of wine and we'll drink a toast. And then we'll see what happens.

One minute later

Re:

Mine has to be a whisky, but apart from that I'm quite happy with your welcome programme. Basically it's no different from your little blindfold number, only without the blindfold and therefore a bit more romantic. Sure, let's do it! Um, are we really going to? Isn't it a bit crazy?

Forty seconds later

Re:

Of course we're really going to do it.

Four minutes later

Re:

But it is risky, Leo. I have no idea whether I'll like the way you kiss. How *do* you kiss? Are you quite firm, or are you soft? Dry or wet? What are your teeth like, are they sharp or blunt? How intrusive and agile is your tongue? Does it feel like hard plastic or foam rubber? Do you keep your eyes open or close them when you kiss? (I suppose if you're blind-tasting it doesn't really matter.) What do you do with your hands? Will you hold me? Where will you hold me, and how firmly? Are you quite quiet, or do you breathe heavily and make noises with your mouth? So tell me, Leo: how do you kiss?

Three minutes later

Re:

I kiss like I write.

Fifty seconds later

Re:

That's incredibly big-headed of you, but it doesn't sound bad at all. Mind you, your writing can be extremely variable.

Forty-five seconds later

Re:

And my kissing can be extremely varied.

Four minutes later

Re:

So long as you promise to kiss me in the same way you've been writing to me yesterday and today, I'll risk it!

Thirty-five seconds later

Re:

Risk it then!

Twelve minutes later

Re:

And what if we want more after we've kissed?

Forty seconds later

Re:

Then we want more.

Fifty seconds later

Re:

And will we do more?

Thirty-five seconds later

Re:

I'm sure we'll know that when the time comes.

Two minutes later

Re:

I hope both of us will know, not just one of us.

Four minutes later

Re:

If one of us knows, the other will too. Only two hours to go, by the way. We should probably stop writing and get ready for our great leap into another dimension. I'm really excited, I have to say.

Eight minutes later

Re:

What should I wear?

One minute later

Re:

I'll leave that up to you.

Fifty-five seconds later

Re:

I'd rather let your fantasy decide.

Two minutes later

Re:

Please don't let my fantasy decide anything. It's running away with me a little right now. But I think you should wear *something*.

Three and a half minutes later

Re:

Should I wear something that might increase the probability of the blinds staying down for a while after we kiss, because neither of us has our hands free?

326

Forty seconds later

Re:

If you don't mind my being succinct: YES!

A minute and a half later

Re:

A 'YES' to a question that demands the answer 'yes' could never be too succinct for me. I'll go and 'brush up' then, as they say. Unless my heart beats its way out of my ribcage, see you at your place in an hour and a half.

Three and a half minutes later

Re:

Press the intercom button marked '15'. When you're in the lift, put in the code 142 and you'll be taken to the top floor. There's only one door up there. It'll be ajar. Then go into the room on the left, just follow the music. Can't wait!

Fifty seconds later

Re:

And I can't wait either. Before we go kissing in the dark, I ought at least to tell you my age:

I'm thirty-four, which is two years younger than you — sorry to point that out.

Two minutes later

Re:

I think I'll have to talk to you properly about 'Boston', Emmi. You've got completely the wrong idea about Boston, or about Boston and me. The whole Boston thing is quite different from how you imagine it. I need to explain that to you. There's so much to say! There's so much to understand. Do you understand?

A minute and a half later

Re:

Slow down, Leo. One thing at a time. Boston can wait. Explanations can wait. Understanding it all can wait. For now let's just kiss. See you soon, my love!

Forty-five seconds later

Re:

See you soon, my love!

10

The following evening

Subject: The north wind

Dear Leo,

I know, it's unforgivable. Your 'silence' is evidence of that. You're not asking why. No, you haven't even asked me why. You're teaching me a lesson. No screaming fit, no attempt to save the situation, no paroxysms of grief. You're not doing anything. You're not saying anything. You let everything wash over you in silence. You don't even ask why. You're behaving as though you knew it all along. And now you're punishing me too. Well, you can't be half as disappointed as I am. Because my disappointment is compounded by my recognition of yours.

I'll tell you why I decided not to come at the very last minute — and I mean it, it really was the very last minute. It was all because of one letter, one single letter in a place where it shouldn't have been, and it came at the worst possible moment. Leo, do you remember you asked me: 'What are you going to tell Bernhard?' And I said, 'I'll tell him I'm meeting up with a friend.' That's exactly what I said to him this evening. 'He'll ask: Do I know him?' — he said exactly that. 'I'll reply: I don't think so, I haven't told you much about him,' — and that was my answer. 'Then I'll say: we've got lots to catch up on so I might be late home!' Those were my very words. 'And he'll say: Have fun,' And he did say that, Leo. But he added one word. He said: 'Have fun, EMMI.' Just the usual 'Have fun', and then he paused. And then came the EMMI. A murmur, no more, and it froze me to the core. He always calls me 'Emma', nothing else. He hasn't called me 'Emmi' for years. I can't even remember the last time he did.

The 'i' instead of the 'a', Leo, that single letter in the wrong place sent shockwaves through me. It was all wrong coming from him. It wasn't his to say. I felt like I'd been stripped bare, the illusion was shattered, it sounded so destructive. As if he could read my thoughts, as if he had seen straight through me. As if he wanted to say: 'I know you want to be 'Emmi', you want to be 'Emmi' all over again. Well, be 'Emmi' then, and have a good time.' I should have said

330

something quite horrible to him in response, I should have said: 'Bernhard, I don't just WANT to be Emmi, I AM Emmi. But I'm not YOUR Emmi. I'm somebody else's. He's never set eyes on me, but he found me. He recognized who I am. He's brought me out of myself. I'm his Emmi. I'm Emmi for Leo. You don't believe me? Well, I can prove it. I have it all in writing.'

I went up to my room. I was going to send you an e-mail, but I couldn't. All I could write was this miserable sentence: 'My dear Leo, I can't come over tonight, it's all too much.' I stared at it for a few moments and then deleted it. I wasn't able to tell you I was going to let you down. It would have been like letting myself down. Something happened, Leo. My soul vanished from the screen. I think I love you. And Bernhard has sensed that. I feel cold. The north wind is blowing. Where can we go from here?

Ten seconds later

Subject: Delivery Status Notification (Returned)

This is an automatically generated Delivery Status Notification.

THIS E-MAIL ADDRESS HAS CHANGED. THE RECIPIENT CAN NO LONGER

RECEIVE MAIL SENT TO THIS ADDRESS. ALL INCOMING MAIL WILL BE DELETED AUTOMATICALLY. FOR ANY QUERIES, PLEASE CONTACT THE SYSTEMS MANAGER.

THE END

We do hope that you have enjoyed reading this large print book.

Did you know that all of our titles are available for purchase?

We publish a wide range of high quality large print books including:
**Romances, Mysteries, Classics
General Fiction
Non Fiction and Westerns**

Special interest titles available in large print are:
**The Little Oxford Dictionary
Music Book
Song Book
Hymn Book
Service Book**

Also available from us courtesy of Oxford University Press:
**Young Readers' Dictionary
(large print edition)
Young Readers' Thesaurus
(large print edition)**

For further information or a free brochure, please contact us at:
**Ulverscroft Large Print Books Ltd.,
The Green, Bradgate Road, Anstey,
Leicester, LE7 7FU, England.
Tel:** (00 44) 0116 236 4325
Fax: (00 44) 0116 234 0205

Other titles published by
The House of Ulverscroft:

DRIFTING SHADOWS

Christina Green

Life on a Dartmoor tenant farm is hard and when Becky Yeo meets Joseph, a travelling labourer and folk-singer, her desire is to change her own life. Then, disobeying her family, she refuses to marry Nat, the farm bailiff. She finds work as a kitchen maid at the Manor House, which harbours a dark mystery concerning her family. Meanwhile, Nat, seeking revenge, blackmails her. When Joseph returns, his love for Becky becomes clear and he must challenge Nat for Becky's hand. But after her secret is revealed, can Becky keep her family together and prevent Joseph from leaving once again?

THE STATISTICAL PROBABILITY OF LOVE AT FIRST SIGHT

Jennifer E. Smith

Stuck at New York's JFK airport, seventeen-year-old Hadley Sullivan faces being late for her father's second wedding in London. And she's not even met her new stepmother. Then, in the waiting area she meets the perfect boy. Oliver is British, with his own reasons for not wanting to return home to London. He's booked in seat 18C. Hadley is in 18A. On the long flight from New York to London they get on very well . . . Unfortunately, landing at Heathrow, Hadley and Oliver lose track of each other in the airport chaos — and she doesn't even know his last name . . .

THE WOUNDED HEART

David Wiltshire

There was no doubt in Lt Mike Gibson's mind that he was going to die. As a lieutenant in the Royal Army Medical Corps, death and carnage had been with him every day from the beaches of Normandy to the crossing of the Rhine. One moment eclipsed all others, in a forest clearing in Germany; where he had the experience of hell on earth. He owed his life to one woman, Lily de Howarth, the woman he adored. And now he was planning to kill her in the name of love . . .

OVER HIS DEAD BODY

Laurie Brown

Ever since Caroline Tucker moved back home from Hollywood to the bright lights of Haven, New Mexico, she's been trying (and failing) to avoid her ex-husband, town sheriff Travis Beaumont. However, she's forced to call him when her niece stumbles across the perfectly preserved body of a cowboy at Girl Scout camp. But is this a crime scene? Or is it just a potential tourist attraction? The mystery of the mummy unravels and Travis digs up some sinister evidence. And the more Caroline tries to keep away from trouble — and Travis — the more they come knocking at her door . . .

ALWAYS THE BRIDE

Jessica Fox

Nobody gets it right all the time. But Zoe Forster always strives for perfection. So when the fortune-teller at her hen party predicts she will marry twice, she's seriously unimpressed. Everyone knows Zoe and Steve are meant to be together. Still, even a marriage made in heaven has to survive in the real world and, a year in, things are getting predictable. Then super-sexy movie star Luke Scottman makes a repeat appearance in Zoe's life, and Zoe and Steve make some unwelcome discoveries about each other's less-than-perfect pasts. It seems the fortune-teller's prediction is about to come true after all . . .